His House of Submission

JUSTINE ELYOT

mischief

Mischief
An imprint of HarperCollins*Publishers*
77–85 Fulham Palace Road,
Hammersmith, London W6 8JB

www.mischiefbooks.com

A Paperback Original 2013

First published in Great Britain in ebook format by
HarperCollins*Publishers* 2012

Copyright © Justine Elyot 2012

Justine Elyot asserts the moral right to
be identified as the author of this work

A catalogue record for this book is
available from the British Library

ISBN-13: 9780007534746

Set in Sabon by FMG using Atomik ePublisher from Easypress

Find out more about HarperCollins and the environment at
www.harpercollins.co.uk/green

Contents

Chapter One

For one tense moment, as I perched with my legs wrapped around Will's hips and his hands clasped beneath my bottom, holding me up, I thought he was going to stagger and fall with me on to the chaise longue.

'Jesus, be careful,' I hissed, still clinging to the open bottle by its expensive neck. 'That's Louis Quinze.'

But thank God for sinewy, strong, horny-handed sons of the soil, because Will recovered his balance and continued in the direction of the drawing-room door, grimly intent on getting me to the bedroom.

'I'll take your word for it,' he said, nudging the door open with his toe and carrying me into the vast hall. 'You're the expert.'

He found the back stairs to the old servants' quarters

and plodded heroically across the parquet.

'I hope you're an expert too,' I said, breathing hotly into his ear. 'And not just when it comes to grounds maintenance.'

'I've never had any complaints.' He smirked and stopped to add another kiss to our already substantial tally. 'All that digging comes in handy when you need to carry women upstairs and throw them on to beds.'

'You've obviously dug a lot.'

'Yeah.'

But once we reached the third flight of steps he had to stop talking and concentrate on the job in hand. On our arrival in his room, with its sloping ceiling and low beams, he was starting to feel the strain, beads of sweat shiny on his forehead.

It was clearly a relief to him when he was able to lower me on to his bed and stand straight, stretching his limbs and grimacing. I could have lived without the grimaces, but this at least gave me the opportunity to run my eyes with avid greed over his body.

Will spent all day, every day, in the open air and it showed, in his healthy tan and his solid build, his broad shoulders and densely packed thighs. He wasn't my usual type at all – sturdy and studly where I usually went for wispy and fey – but two weeks cooped up in this place with no other company had worked its erotic magic on me and now I thirsted for him.

2

He fell to his knees on the mattress, towering over me, giving me the full roguish glint.

'So now I've got you in my lair, Sarah ...' he whispered.

'Your lair, eh? Your eyrie, high above the park.'

I propped myself on an elbow and put the wine bottle down on the bedside table.

'Something like that.' He put a hand on my collarbone and pushed me roughly back down.

'You sound as if you're the hunter and I'm your prey,' I said, reaching out and grabbing his wrist. 'But I'm not sure you've got it the right way around.'

He swung one leg around so that he straddled me and pinned me down with my wrists above my head.

'I'm pretty sure I have,' he said, leaning down low to rasp the words into my ear. 'Aren't you?'

Enjoying the feeling of restraint I twisted and turned and tried to buck him off me, knowing I wouldn't succeed, not wanting to succeed, but wanting the resistance, the friction, the arousing sense of powerlessness it all led to.

He chuckled, understanding the game and its unspoken rules, and held me all the firmer.

'No way, Sarah,' he taunted, releasing one wrist and catching both in one hand, just to show me that he could. 'Now I've got you where I want you, I'm not letting you go.'

'You planned this, then?'

He shut me up with a kiss, a fierce stamp of his lips on mine. His free hand closed around the neckline of my shirt then undid the top three buttons.

'Of course I did. I've been watching you. Ever since you came here.'

More buttons slid open, then Will's rough palm was on my bare skin, beneath my bra cups, gliding over my ribs and stomach.

'Nobody else to look at, is there?' I whispered, but I was starting to lose the capacity for repartee, especially when his mouth descended on my neck, then the hollow of my throat, then my cleavage.

The heaving of my chest and my little moan of pleasure must have given him the clue that it would be safe to release my wrists. I colluded with him now instead of fighting him. We were working together in the pursuit of pleasure. And this was where things always became a little awkward for me.

I was so anxious to be 'good in bed' – to be active and passionate and skilled – that I lost all grip on what I was feeling myself.

Objectively I knew that he was sucking on my nipple and it should feel good – it did feel good – but the feeling good was layered beneath my own worries about what I was doing to make him feel good. A former lover had enjoyed it when I massaged the back of his neck at times like these. Would that be a good move? I tried it. He seemed to appreciate it. Or was I irritating him and he was just too polite to say so? Not that he could say much, with a mouthful of nipple. Oh, God. It was too difficult. I couldn't disconnect, could never go with the flow. If only the flow would just come and take me, throw me up on its racing tide and carry me, swirling in white water, into the depths where real, unforced pleasure lay. I knew it existed. History showed that it was real. Why couldn't it ever be real for me?

His head rose, his eyes peering at me from above my breasts.

'Bloody bras,' he muttered. 'Whoever invented them wants shooting.'

He plucked at the underwires until I obligingly sat up and unhooked it myself. I looked down at my breasts, amazed at how much larger my nipples could grow, then turned my face back to Will when he cupped them and rubbed his thumbs around the sensitive nubs.

'I hope it didn't kill the moment too much,' I said apologetically.

'Sh, don't be daft. The removal of the bra is a rite of passage. I'm used to it.'

'I bet you are.' I reached out for his T-shirt, pulling it out of his jeans waistband. He followed my cue and removed it himself, his arms stretching up away from an expanse of mouthwateringly taut chest above a flat abdomen, everything where it should be. His skin was golden and he had a tattoo on his right bicep, one of those Celtic knots encompassing the muscle.

'I like your tattoo. Celtic blood?'

'Nah. Everyone was having these done back then.'

He flexed his arm then pounced back down, his nose hovering millimetres above mine.

'You don't have any little surprises for me, then? Tattoos? Piercings?' His fingers drifted over my nipples, my navel, towards my trousers, under the waist …

'No, no,' I gasped, before he came to land, palm-first, in my pubic bristles. Damn. Why had I not realised I was going to let him seduce me tonight? I squirmed, pulling my lower body away from his explorations. 'Nothing like that.'

'Hey, hey.' He held up his hand, his lower lip jutting a little. 'It's OK if you don't want to –'

'I do want to. It's just … I didn't wax.'

'Oh God, do you think I care about that?' He shook his head and set to unfastening my buttons. 'You can perm it and dye it pink for all I care.'

The trousers were yanked off, followed by my knickers.

He put his hand, sideways on, between my lips, as he gazed down at my unclothed pussy.

'As long as it's wet and ready for me …' he murmured.

I hoped I was. Was I? I couldn't really tell, too much performance anxiety muffling the sensation, warping my sensual urges.

He bent lower, pattering, remarkably delicately, on my clit with his thick, callused fingers.

'Nice and warm,' he breathed.

I sat up and reached for his belt, but he batted me away.

'Hey,' he said, slightly reproachful, and I blushed in agony at making a wrong move. 'I want to pay attention to you first. It's not a game of tit-for-tat. Relax.'

Relax. Yeah. Nothing like asking the impossible.

'Relaxation doesn't come easily to me,' I muttered, still mortified.

'No kidding.' He kissed my forehead, then my lips, then he patted my cheek sympathetically. 'Just try, eh? For me.'

I tried. I lay back and shut my eyes and channelled all my awareness towards his fingers and my clit. His touch was rough but sure, but he didn't say anything, leaving too much silence so that the ticking of his clock and the strange gurgles of the hot-water pipes intruded. How did it feel? How would I describe it?

'You are enjoying this, aren't you?' he said, sounding puzzled.

'Yes, but ... can you just fuck me?'

His fingers stopped what they were doing and he drew them out.

'Sure,' he said.

My eyes were still screwed shut. I heard the sound of his belt coming off, then his jeans.

'Most girls like a bit of foreplay,' he said.

'I'm just … it's been a long time. I want to remember what it feels like.'

I heard the opening and shutting of drawers then the snap of rubber.

'OK. This is what it feels like. You could open your eyes, you know.'

'I like to keep them shut.'

'Didn't realise I was that hard to look at.'

'It's not you. Please …'

My plea was answered by the blunt arrival of a rounded cock head between my legs. His heat and scent moved down close to me, wrapping me in them, taking me out of my isolation, making me want him now. I put my hands on his shoulders, shivering pleasurably at the way they flexed and moved underneath his skin. He was so strong. I wanted him to make this hard, make it fast, pile-drive into me, obliterate my senses.

'Please,' I whispered.

He thrust forward, just the forceful way I wanted it.

'Yeah?' he said. 'That what you want? That good enough for you?'

'Oh, yes. More. Please. More.'

I opened my eyes and looked at his forearms, braced either side of my shoulders. How tense and powerful they were, holding him steady while he worked me. His chest heaved up and down, brushing my nipples with each jerking motion. He was handsome and he was fucking me. I was being fucked. What did it feel like?

It felt like a series of shocks, stretching my hidden channel, a jolt jolt jolt. I looked for the sense of being overpowered, but as always, I looked too hard and couldn't quite place it.

I tried to reach out for it.

'I need this,' I said.

'Yeah,' he agreed, panting with exertion. 'You need this. You've been needing it ever since you got here. Keep those legs wide, baby, cos you'll be getting more and more of it.'

Yes. This was working now. This was moving me towards my goal. He had been watching me, seeing the desperate slut inside the Peter Pan collars, he had known all along that what I needed was to be pinned down and given a good seeing-to. He understood what would keep me sweet and it amounted to being kept on my back with my thighs spread, taking plenty of hot, hard, grimy, sweaty fucking. He would give it to me and then he would tell his friends and they would give it to me and then ...

I was almost there. I slipped my fingers between our grinding pelvises and touched the spot, my hand immediately hot and damp.

His cock was a nice one, firm and substantial, if not quite in proportion with his godlike body. My knuckles grazed against the root of it, feeling it rub back and forth, the rubber soaked and slippery now.

He plunged and plunged and I felt my buttocks tense and my spine arch and oh, yes.

'Oh, yes,' I said it out loud, again and again and, just as I crested the high point and tipped back down the other side of the wave, I said, 'Thank you, Sir.'

And then I turned my head away and considered smacking myself in the face. Why on earth had I said that out loud?

But Will didn't question it, simply banged away all the more until his own orgasm ripped through his body – really, I could feel the ripping – and then collapsed on top of me.

I always liked this moment, the hammering of twin hearts and the gathering of breath. Somehow this was a better payoff than the preceding orgasms.

'You came, didn't you?' panted Will, rolling off eventually.

'You heard me, didn't you? Of course I did. Of course.' I stroked his close-cropped hair. Beneath it, his scalp felt hot.

'Just ... you're a bit of a strange fruit, aren't you?'

'What do you mean?'

'What you said. When you came.'

I turned my face away.

'Don't make fun of me.'

'I'm not. Sarah, honestly, I'm not. Look at me. Talk to me.'

I dared a glance from beneath low-slung eyelids. He didn't look jokey or mocking. I opened them wider.

'You and him,' Will said. 'You'd probably get on.'

'Him? Jasper Jay?'

I couldn't refer to my employer by anything but his full name. We weren't on first-name terms yet. Indeed, we weren't on any terms. We had never met.

'Yeah. Jasper Almighty Jay.'

'You don't like him?'

'He's all right. He pays me.'

'What's he like?'

'Didn't he interview you?'

'No. It was a woman, his secretary or PA or something. He was in France, filming. Well, he still is. Anyway, why did you say that we'd get on?'

'That thing you said. It was a bit kinky.'

'Sorry.'

'Shut up apologising, you daft ha'p'orth. Absolutely nothing wrong with a bit of kink. It was quite a turn-on, as it goes.'

I exhaled gratefully. I hadn't made such a prize exhibition of myself after all. Though I could still see, in the corner of my mind, a little mental film reel of Will down at the local pub regaling his mates with the story.

'Thanks. So?'

'So. Jasper Jay and you might have a little something in common.'

'What do you mean? He's into …?'

'Get your kit back on,' whispered Will, 'or not, as you choose, and I'll show you.'

I couldn't really be bothered with all the jeans and bra palaver, so I borrowed a threadbare towelling robe of Will's and followed my half-dressed lover out of the bedroom.

'He hired you to catalogue his collections,' said Will, creeping barefoot down the back stairs. 'But I wonder if he meant you to see this one.'

'A collection?' I whispered. Why was I whispering? Why were we creeping? It all felt deeply illicit.

We tiptoed past the library, with its vast collection of first editions, some of which I'd managed to list. Past the drawing room and the morning room and all the other rooms, chock-full of antiques and artefacts. Up the main stairs to the first floor bedrooms, past my little bolthole and into …

'Oh, I don't think we should go into his room.'

'Why not? He isn't here. He'll never know. Here, have a swig.'

He passed me the bottle of expensive red wine, but I was too wary of spilling it, and besides, my mind was occupied with taking in the huge four-poster bed and the dark oak furnishings and the gigantic chest that took up at least a fifth of the large room's space.

Will took a key from his jeans back pocket and fitted it into the chest's lock.

'This is his private stuff,' I agonised. 'I don't think we should.'

Too late, though, because the lid was raised and I stared down into an abyss of deviance.

'God,' I whispered, lowering myself to my knees and peering inside. It was all so neatly compartmentalised, boxes within boxes, but some of the contents were in long fabric bags. For instance, the whips. And canes. And riding crops.

'Is this what you're into?' asked Will, opening one of the boxes and showing me a selection of cuffs – leather, metal, fur-lined, velcro, you name it.

'This is ... I mean. Wow. It's a collection. Does he just collect the stuff or does he use it?'

I opened another box, my curiosity overwhelming my caution now, and found a selection of first-edition titles, some of which – like The Story of O– were familiar to me, others not so well known.

'The Harem of the Flagellants,' I read, my finger hovering over a cheaply but sturdily bound Victorian tome. I shivered.

It was one thing to fantasise about these things, but quite another to see them in real life. I felt a strange kind of fear, as if I had skimmed a surface and been dragged underneath it. Now I was here in the underworld, could I get out again?

Will hadn't answered my question, so I asked it again.

'Does any of this stuff get used?'

'I don't know. He hasn't had anyone here for a while. When he stays here, he just buries himself. Doesn't go out. It's like hibernation.'

'I guess his work is quite intense. Ever since he won the Palme d'Or.'

Will shrugged.

'Don't ask me. I've worked here for four years but I wouldn't say I knew him. This is the closest I've got to knowing anything about him. This here.' He waved his hand at the boxes.

I had opened another. It contained things I had never seen in my life before, silicone things that were a little bit like dildoes but with an outward flare halfway along the length.

'What the hell are these?'

Will snorted.

'Don't you know?'

'I've never done anything kinky,' I defended myself.

'Butt plugs, my love,' he said, picking one up.

'Oh, don't touch it!'

'Why not?'

I shook my head. I knew I was panicking, but I couldn't seem to rein myself in.

'Fingerprints,' I mumbled.

He burst out laughing at that, waving the butt plug in the air.

'You're funny,' he said, between fresh gusts of mirth.

'You'll have to share the joke.' A third voice spoke from the doorway.

I fell backwards on to my arse, my hand clamping my mouth so hard and fast I almost knocked a couple of teeth out.

I watched through wide-stretched eyes as everything seeming to crash into slo-mo. Will dropped the butt plug and raised himself to his feet, shoulders back, squared for combat.

The man in the door was, presumably, Jasper Jay, though he wasn't the way I remembered him from that medical soap he used to be in when I was a girl. Of course, a lot of water had passed under the bridge since then – fifteen years' worth. He wasn't a fresh-faced bright-eyed youth in a white coat now. He stood with one arm braced against the doorframe, in an expensive suit, its light biscuit colour accentuating his dark looks. He had that famous-person thing of looking somehow bigger and shinier and brighter than a real man. I hadn't fancied him in the medical soap, or in the many news clips of him accepting the Palme d'Or, but now I could almost see the vortex of charisma inside which he existed.

But now wasn't a good time to be ogling my boss.

Now was about the worst time ever for that kind of thing.

'Shit, I thought you were in France,' was Will's pretty dreadful attempt at defending his actions.

I remained silent, cowering on a Turkish rug of early nineteenth-century vintage, concentrating on keeping Will's bathrobe tightly wrapped around me.

'Shit, you're fired,' replied Jay laconically.

'You can't just –'

'Yes, I can. Pack your things. Load up your car. Get out of here.'

'But my rights ...'

'In what universe isn't this gross misconduct?' He stepped into the room, unfolding his arm grandly to usher Will through the door. 'Not ours, at least. Goodbye. I'll forward any holiday entitlement you had outstanding on to you.'

'Mr Jay, please ... four years of good service.'

'Ruined in the space of one night.' Jay shook his head. 'Like a film script, isn't it?' There was a pause. 'I can't help noticing that you're still here.'

Will looked at me, as if expecting me to leap to his passionate defence. Seeing this wasn't about to happen, he made as dignified an exit as he could muster.

I watched the knots between his shoulder blades, the buzz-cut V at his nape, retreat through the door.

I looked up, expecting my neck to be next on the block.

I ought to say something but I couldn't think what so

I waited, while tension and mortification played ping-pong in my emotional centre.

He didn't say anything either, which was odd. He just looked at me, not angrily or severely, just sort of … pensively. His eyes were wintry and sombre, but not hard.

His abstraction was only broken when I cleared my throat and swallowed, looking desperately around me for any magical escape route that might present itself.

'Sit down,' he said.

I was already sitting down, but I gathered from the direction of his waving hand that I was to go and sit on the side of the bed.

There were armchairs in the room, but these wouldn't do, it seemed.

'Are you going to sack me too?' I asked, the words coming out of my cotton-wool mouth in a thick wad.

He made no reply but walked over to the chest and reached inside.

I'd lost track of my heart. It had giddied up and up and now it was steeplechasing fit to collapse. What on earth did he have in mind?

He drew out one of the many long, thin boxes and came to stand over me, a looming presence, shadowing me. I felt very small and very vulnerable and yet a part of me was revelling in my disgrace, making sure it recalled all the details to be mulled over at leisure later.

17

He took the lid off the box and withdrew the contents – a wide strap of supple leather, with stiffer, darker, embossed leather at one end and a metal chain link intended for hanging it on a hook.

'Do you know what this is?' He presented it across his two palms where it lay, dormant but no less deadly, its antique tang gathering in my senses and whipping them up. 'Take it. Hold it.'

Uncertainly, I plucked the thing from him and read the gilt lettering on the leather handle. 'Holborn Barbering Supplies'. The leather was cold and smooth and cruelly sensual to the touch.

'Well?' Jay's voice was soft but commanding.

'It's a razor strop. Antique.'

'Can you date it?'

'Not precisely. Mid-Victorian, perhaps.'

'It's not modern.'

'No, it's too heavy to be modern.'

'That's right. You know about these things, don't you, Sarah?'

I looked up sharply at his use of my given name, which was spoken in a peculiarly intimate tone, with a whisper of caress behind it.

'I … you hired me, after all.'

'Yes, I did. I hired you.'

'Do I still …?' I couldn't finish the sentence.

'Have a job here?' He stepped back and looked up at

the ceiling, seeking advice in its elaborate cornicing and plaster rose. 'Yes, I think you do.'

I waited a moment for my breathing to regulate then said, 'Thank you.'

The silence between us was broken by the sound of bags being thrown heavily down the stairs.

'Excuse me one moment,' he said, leaving the room, presumably to direct the departure of Will. I wondered if Jasper Jay directed everything in his life like this, getting the details right, making art of the day-to-day. He had certainly orchestrated our first encounter to make it memorable. I stared down at the antique strop, picturing it employed for other purposes than the sharpening of blades. Had he used this on somebody? Had it fallen heavy on some bent-over bottom, marking it with a hot red rectangle?

I heard the front door slam, the revving of an engine outside. I wondered if I should feel sorrier for Will, but I couldn't summon much in the way of sympathy when it came down to it. He'd been caught fair and square with his hand in the ... well, I could hardly call it a cookie jar.

Jasper came back, but he didn't enter the room, just stood with his hands on the top of the doorframe, leaning in, looking me up and down and over until I bristled with a weird exhilaration. At least the towelling robe was thick and he couldn't see the way my nipples perked into stiffness under his gaze.

'Come downstairs,' he said at last. 'I'll light the fire. Have a drink with me.'

'Oh … this robe … I should get dressed …'

'No, you shouldn't.'

I stood up and dithered with the razor strop, mutely asking him what to do with it.

'Bring it with you.'

He walked off and I followed him, the leather clutched to my chest, trying to make my footsteps as barely-there as possible on the highly polished wood.

He had lit the fire by the time I reached the sitting room. I winced at the sight of the two abandoned wine glasses on the low coffee table. Jasper picked one up and sniffed into it.

'Christ, the fucking nerve of him,' he muttered. 'My best vintage.' But when he put it down, he smiled at me, a dazzling, film-star smile that knocked me off course.

'Sarah,' he said, all effusiveness and warmth. 'Sit down.'

I sat on one side of the fire while he poured me some wine from an ornate cut-glass decanter, circa 1820s.

'Aren't you angry with me?' I asked, taking a nerving sip while he seated himself in the opposite wing-backed chair with his own glass.

'I'm assuming you were led astray,' he said.

'You're assuming?'

'Yes. Because that's the interpretation that suits me. So I'm sticking to it.'

I hid my confusion in another sip.

'You can leave if you really want, of course. But I'd prefer it if you stayed. I went to some considerable lengths to find you, Sarah. Now you're here, I have no intention of letting you go.'

'What?'

I put the glass on the card table and sat up straight. What could he possibly mean by that? The fire burned at the side of my face and I put my hand up to my cheek, protecting it.

'The job you applied for wasn't universally advertised, you know. I only had it placed in the university history department magazine I knew you wrote for.'

'What?' I said again.

I thought back to the advertisement, quite a showy one for my humble little student history-geek mag. I'd presumed it to be just one of many, fired off to every university history department in the country.

'After I read that article of yours.'

'You read an article of mine? In Past Pleasures?'

This made no sense at all. Why the actual hell would famous arthouse film director Jasper Jay read my obscure little postgraduate pamphlet?

'Yes. Don't look so shocked.' He laughed. 'It was forwarded to me by an associate who thought it ... up my street. As it were. And it was. It was an amazing article. Superbly researched and lacking the usual prurient or hysterical tone one grows so weary of.'

'You're talking about … I can't remember what I called it …'

' "The Old Perversity Shop". About that collection of Victorian fetish implements they found in Lincoln last year.'

I looked into the fire, wanting to laugh for some reason. This was like a dream, unravelling so quickly and so absurdly.

'The thing about your article, Sarah,' he said softly, 'is that it was written with more than academic curiosity. It was written with enthusiasm. With love.'

'You think so?'

'I know so. Only somebody close to the subject could have written about it in the way you did. No "ugh, those old-school freaks". No "isn't this interesting, in a scholarly, abstract kind of way, of course". You understood the allure of those whips and cuffs. Didn't you?'

I was under the spotlight, on the spot. There was no feasible response to this other than a good deal of squirming and evasive body language.

But something told me that Jasper Jay wasn't a man who would stand for squirming and evasive body language.

'Didn't you?' he persisted. 'There's no point trying to deny it. I see it in you.'

'Do you mean to say that you read my article, placed the advert in the hope that I'd respond and, and …?'

'Had you hired on the spot? Yes. My agent knew she had to give the job to Sarah Wells. So when Sarah Wells walked into the office ... bingo.'

He clicked his fingers and beamed with delight.

My toes were curled right under and I realised that every muscle in my body was held in a state of supreme tautness, as if in preparation for some kind of desperate death-match. Did it mean I was scared? I didn't feel scared. Not exactly.

'But why?'

'You've seen my collection. I had hoped to leave it until later in the summer, when you'd finished the more ... orthodox ... portion of your task and my filming schedule was complete, but it can't be helped, can it? Even my strict timetable can be subject to sudden changes.'

'Why did you come back? I thought you were in France till August.'

'So did I.' He sighed, sipped his wine. 'Our leading man disagreed. Ridiculous bastard went and got his leg broken in a jetski accident. Next movie I make, I'm having everyone, cast and crew, living in a barracks and having to apply to me for passes to get out.'

'Control-freaky.'

He smiled at me again.

'Yes.'

I appeared to have finished the wine. Christ, that was

quick. I needed to sip from the glass, for my hands to have something to do besides shaking.

'Don't be nervous,' he said. I watched his fingers, long and white, stroke the stem of his glass. 'Unless you want to be.'

'I can't help it,' I said, a tad mutinously. 'This situation isn't covered in Emily Post. I don't know what to say or do, or …'

'Just say what you feel. Do what you feel.'

'In that case –' I put the glass down with an overstated flourish '– I'm going to bed.'

He shrugged and smiled, watching me make as dignified an exit as I could.

'Sweet dreams,' he said when I reached the door.

I looked back at him. His face was shadowed, his brow low, the smile a Hollywood-white tease.

I fled.

Chapter Two

I turned the key in my door lock and sat down on the bed, catching my breath. Situation out of control. I had to try and slot the different pieces of the night into place, discipline them into making some kind of sense.

One: I shagged Will.

Two: Will showed me Jasper's collection of BDSM gear.

Three: Jasper caught us and fired Will.

Four: It turns out he hired me because I wrote that article.

My mental cataloguing stopped here, unable to proceed.

He hired me because I wrote that article.

Jasper Jay, the film director and winner of the Palme

d'Or, had read my silly little piece on Victorian kinksters and hired me on the strength of it.

Why had he gone to those lengths? Weren't there professional evaluators of this kind of thing? Could he not have got somebody from an auction house?

I felt creeped out, as if he had stalked me, which, in a way, he had. Where was the boundary between stalking and headhunting anyway?

What did he really want?

I lay down and let my thoughts drift around my head. The sensible course was clear. Tomorrow I would pack my bags and leave. This was all too weird and potentially disastrous. Shame about the money though and ...

Practicalities grew vaguer, blurring away. I still held the razor strop in my hand and its particular heft and texture beguiled me into fantasy. Jasper Jay, in Victorian times, my Victorian husband, with impressive sideburns and a cravat, sharpening his razor on the leather.

Me on the bed, in my bodice and pantalettes, trying to fasten my corset.

'You should get Jenny to do that for you,' he says, and I watch his hands move as he plies the blade, swipe, swipe, swipe, from the top to the bottom.

'That's what I meant to tell you, dearest,' I say, and my voice shakes. I'm nervous.

He puts down the razor, one eyebrow raised.

'My love?'

'Jenny ... and I ... that is to say ... we had a difference of opinion.'

'Oh?' I watch his fist close around the strop.

'It was nothing really but I'm afraid I lost my temper.'

'Have we not discussed your impetuous humours?' The question is couched so gently, so reasonably, but my heart jumps to my throat.

We have many such discussions. Discussions that don't involve a great deal of actual discussion.

'I know, dearest. But I'm afraid I lost my head for one moment and I ... slapped her.'

He sighs, lowers his head, puts a hand to his brow. He is at the end of his tether, I know, and I have worked so hard on my self-discipline, but we both know that my impulses overpower my will too often.

'And she has left?' he says in a low voice.

'I'm afraid she has, dearest.'

'And she will explain the circumstances to the agency and we shall be on their black list. Another black list.'

I cannot deny it. I fidget with my corset laces, wrapping them round and around my finger.

'Shall we discuss this now?' I ask in a small voice.

'Oh, yes, I think the more immediate the consequence, the more beneficial the lesson, don't you?'

'Yes, dearest.'

He waits for me. I know what I have to do. I remove the corset and take my place at the foot of the bed, gripping the carved wooden footboard for grim life. I hear the little clink of metal as he removes the strop from its hook.

'Now, my love,' he says, pacing behind me. 'You know I never get angry with you and I am not angry now. I know, however, that you are angry with yourself, aren't you?'

'Yes, dearest.'

I tilt my pelvis forward, bend a little at the knees.

'And in order for you to forgive yourself, the matter must be dealt with so that you can feel refreshed and prepared for a new start. Is that not so?'

'It is so, dearest. Oh, I am so sorry to disappoint you.'

'I will admit to some disappointment, Sarah, and some sorrow that we find ourselves once again in this position. Let this punishment be swift and sharp and then all can be forgiven, if not forgotten.'

Not for a few days, at least. Every time I sit.

He steps forward and parts the cloth of my drawers, the split exposing my bottom. His hand is sure and firm. I hear the shush of the strop rubbing against his trousers, dangling from his other hand.

I should not admit to my faults while he is shaving. I must learn to pick a time when that strop is far out of his reach. Perhaps on the way to church on Sundays.

I will pay for my ill-timed confession now. I squeeze shut my eyes and lower my head, trying to relax my neck muscles.

Oh, the sound it makes, the mighty whoosh, the burning crack of impact. It is so heavy and yet so fiendishly flexible. It snaps across my poor posterior, over and again, marking me with shame, making my skin blush.

As my husband whips me, he lectures me on my shortcomings and how they must be overcome. He points out his position in society and at his place of employment and how I must be a credit to him and our home and family. He reminds me of my position, my vow of obedience, my promise of submission.

And the strop catches me in every painful place it can until I scorch beneath its scorpion tongue.

'Enough,' he says, his voice laden with exertion. 'I trust that the lesson is well inculcated.'

'Very well, Sir,' I whisper.

'Good. Then let us forgive.'

After the discussion, there is always forgiveness. He shows it by placing the strop beneath my breasts and holding it there while he lowers his trousers and underwear and places his manhood between my nether lips.

He bathes it in my dew, noting well how it flows, for he knows how these discussions excite me. He plunges hard into my tight heat, stretching my cunny wide, slapping his thighs up against my sore bottom. But this rough usage is no punishment, oh, no, it melts into the purest pleasure. He holds the strap against my breasts while he thrusts, its well-worn surface rubbing against those tender buds.

29

He takes me well and thoroughly, until I sob with a presentiment of the flood to follow, and then he puts the strap between my legs and presses it to my pearl and then, oh, yes, oh, my dearest love …

I opened my eyes and then sat up straight. Oh, what the bloody hell was I thinking? The real strop, the antique, possibly worth a shedload of money, was pressed to my clit, all shiny and slick with my juices.

I grabbed a tissue and rubbed it clean, but when I put it to my face and sniffed, my scent and the leather were all mixed in one incredibly sexual cocktail. What if I'd destroyed the delicate balance of the textile? Did I not know better than to masturbate with precious artefacts? History 101, surely. Though I didn't remember seeing it in the textbook.

I put the strop aside and began packing. It seemed my only course.

*   *   *

'What's that?'

Jasper at the breakfast table in the cavernous kitchen, laconic, handsome, dangerous.

I put my bags down on the trestle.

'I think I ought to go.'

'Why?' He bit into a triangle of toast.

'Um, because I don't really know what's going on.'

'And you like to know what's going on, do you, Sarah?'

'Generally speaking.'

'You don't like stories?'

'I don't … follow.'

He patted the chair beside him and for some reason I didn't think twice about going over there and sitting down.

'Do you or don't you? Like stories?'

'Well, yes, I do.'

'Do you always know what's going on in a story?'

'Sometimes. If it's blatantly signposted, I suppose. More often not.'

'It's dull, isn't it, when you know the ending.'

'Not always.' I had an idea what he might be driving at. 'I can watch film versions of classic novels over and over, even though I know the ending.'

'That's a different kind of pleasure,' he said.

'Maybe.'

'The thing is, Sarah, if you know the ending, you can't explore any other possibilities. If you know what's going on, you can't be surprised. You can't have your breath taken away. You miss all the best bits. Do you see?'

I swallowed. He was very close to me and I was intensely conscious of it. So intensely conscious that I was having some difficulty processing thought.

'You're very …'

He leaned closer.

'Very what?'

31

'Very … I don't know.'

'Don't go, Sarah. If you don't go, I'll make you bacon and eggs.'

Breakfast. Probably a good idea.

'That would be … acceptable,' I said.

'And I know you're an accepting person,' he said, rising and moving towards the cooker top. 'An open-minded soul.' He opened up a pack of bacon. 'Incidentally, do you have my razor strop?'

Oh, God. I thought of it on my bedside table, still perfumed with essence de Sarah.

He turned around, my silence putting him on the scent. 'Sarah?'

'Oh. Yeah.'

'You're scarlet.'

'Am I?'

'Is there something you want to tell me?' He threw the bacon in the pan, never taking his eyes from me.

'I don't …' No, I didn't want to tell him. But perhaps I ought to. But then what? What would he do or say? A tremor quickened in my lower stomach, a tightening at my core.

'Well?'

'It's just … I spilled something on it. I'm sorry. I'll get it professionally cleaned.' What was I saying? Was I really going to explain what had happened to some remote tradesperson?

'Bring it down,' he said.

'Now?'

He nodded, the corners of his mouth tight.

My legs were heavy on the ascent of the staircase, and I felt sick with panic, yet at the same time exhilarated, as if I were embarking on some fantastic adventure.

When I sniffed the leather, my faint hope that the aroma had faded overnight was dashed. Maybe Jasper wouldn't notice. But no. That was just exactly the kind of thing he would notice. In fact, he probably knew what had happened already. I had the feeling he could see inside me, peel away my layers and pluck out my private thoughts.

I put its metal ring around my finger and let it dangle on my way back downstairs. All the beautiful pictures watched me pass, all the ballerinas, bons vivants, burlesque girls. They were the witnesses to my onward march of shame.

Jasper was breaking eggs into the pan when I re-entered the kitchen.

'Ah,' he said, looking up. 'Show me.'

He held out the hand that wasn't occupied with pushing the bacon around with a spatula.

I laid the strop across his palm, tenderly, giving it the respect I had forgotten to accord it last night.

He put down the spatula and inspected the strop at close quarters.

33

'Where's the spillage?' he asked.

It wasn't visible but I pointed towards the damned spot.

He frowned.

'I don't see anything. What did you spill?'

He bent closer and then drew in a breath, raising his eyes to mine. I held myself perfectly still for a horrible second, then he smiled the most radiant smile I had ever seen.

'Oh, I see,' he said.

I had nothing to say. I stood there, panting a little, wondering why my legs wouldn't let me run away.

He wrapped it around his hand, slowly, making sure I paid attention.

'What shall we do about this?' he wondered aloud.

'I can get it cleaned,' I repeated.

'No, no.' He shook his head. 'I'll take care of that. That wasn't what I meant.'

With a tremor of shock, it occurred to me that I had been meaning to leave, so all of this was technically avoidable. The thought crashed into my head but I didn't want to let it in. I didn't want to leave now. I wanted to know what was going to happen. I wanted to read the next page of the story.

'What did you mean then?' I whispered.

'What am I going to do with you?'

The pan hissed and spat behind him. He sighed and

turned his attention to it, putting down the strop and picking up the spatula.

'Sit down,' he said. 'No, before you do that, take your bloody bags back upstairs.'

I wanted to ask him what he was going to do with me, since the words hung so agonisingly and tantalisingly between us, but I did as I was told instead, running up the stairs two at a time and flinging the bags on the bed.

Anything could happen, I told myself, racing back down. Anything could happen and I want it to!

The plates were on the table and he was already digging into his food.

'You look like you could do with a square meal,' he said. 'There's nothing in the cupboards. What have you been living on?'

'Soup, mainly,' I said, sliding into the chair opposite him.

'Not that foul packet stuff I saw on the shelf?'

'Yeah.' I felt guilty for my consumption of powdered soup. Obviously it was the Wrong Thing to do.

'That won't do. You're going to need your strength, my girl.'

Jesus, what was happening to me? Lightning bolts, electricity up and down my spine and all over my skin. As for my crotch, I could barely sit still, it felt so full of sparks.

'Am I? For ... what you're going to do with me?'

35

'All that cataloguing,' he said, deadpan. 'Takes it out of you, I imagine.'

'Please,' I said. 'If you're going to … make me pay … can you tell me how?'

'Later,' he said. 'Eat your eggs. You need protein.'

He refused to refer to the subject again, questioning me instead on my background and education until the food and the mugs of strong tea were all gone.

I wanted to talk about him, since his experiences were so much more interesting than mine, but I sensed that he didn't take well to interrogation and would dispense information at his own pace. I watched him speak, watched the light and shade fall across his face, followed the expressive motions of his hands. All his animation seemed to be channelled into them, while his facial expressions remained serene and controlled. He is master of himself, I thought, and that made me want to squirm even more.

'Finished?' he asked when I laid down my knife and fork.

'Yes, thanks.'

'You'd better get to work then. Go on. I'll wash up.'

I hesitated. Wasn't he going to mention the strop débâcle?

'What room are you working in at the moment?' he asked.

'The, uh, the one with the piano.'

'The drawing room,' he corrected me. 'I'll be in the study. Come and wait outside in, shall we say, two hours? That'll give me enough time to devise something suitable.'

Instant shivers. *Something suitable.*

'Run along then, Sarah,' he said with a ghoulish smile. 'We mustn't neglect our work, must we?'

But I'm afraid I did neglect my work.

Over and over again I came to with a start, some ornament or other in my hand, after drifting into reverie. If I carried on like that, something was going to get broken. And then what might be my fate? I kept going to the door and looking around it, towards the study, listening. Sometimes I could hear his voice, faintly, making telephone calls, or the tap of a keyboard.

While he worked, he was thinking of me. Thinking of what was to be done with me, for my shameless behaviour with his property.

And while I worked, I was thinking of him. Thinking of how he compelled and disturbed and attracted and repelled me. I had never met a man who could do all those things simultaneously before. Perhaps there was no other man in the world who could.

The hands of all the antique clocks made their slow progress through time until the two hours had elapsed and I put down my clipboard and pencil, patted down my skirt and left the room.

I could keep walking, walk to the front door, walk to the car, get in the car, drive away.

But I stopped at the study door and lifted my hand and …

I heard his chair creak.

I knocked.

He didn't reply.

I knocked again.

'Come in.'

The study was a glorious room and his desk was one of my favourite pieces in the whole house. Mahogany with brass handles and a green leather writing area in the shape of a cross, on top of which his computer looked somewhat incongruous. He should be writing longhand with parchment and ink. There was a raised gallery at the back of the desk, along which were perched a procession of film awards, the Palme d'Or in pride of place.

I breathed in the beeswax and stillness, letting it calm my jangling nerves.

'Sarah,' he said, sitting back in his oxblood leather chair. 'Now we come to the real test.'

'Do we?'

He opened a drawer and brought out the strop. I chewed on the inside of my cheek, staring at it.

'When I was at university,' he said, 'I directed a Gilbert and Sullivan opera. The Mikado. Do you know it?'

'Yes,' I said, discombobulated by this line of conversation.

'There's a song in it about how the Mikado dispenses justice. He's particularly keen, he says, to let the punishment fit the crime. I like his way of thinking.'

He stroked a finger along the strop. My eyes followed it, hypnotised.

'I see,' I said, filling in the tense space with the useless remark.

'So what punishment do you think would fit your crime, Sarah?'

He smiled up at me, for all the world as if he had asked me what flavour ice-cream I preferred.

'I think you're the Mikado around here. I think it's your decision.'

'Ah, my decision. Yes. That's a good answer. And I like the bit about being the Mikado too. The emperor. Monarch of all I survey.' He tapped his fingertips on the strop, then picked it up and slapped the end into his palm. 'How far has your interest in this kind of thing gone?'

'This kind of thing ... meaning ...'

'You know what I mean. What have you actually done? If anything.'

'Nothing. I've only ...'

'Fantasised?'

'Written about it,' I said defiantly.

'Ah,' he said, leaning back in his chair. 'I thought you might know the score. You've played this so well, like an old hand. But you're new to it all. And, lucky for you, I'm not. You do want to try it, don't you?'

'I've always wanted to.'

There. I had crossed a line now. I had delivered myself right into his hands.

'Good. Come over here then.'

He put the strop back on the desk as I drew level with him and he placed his hands on my hips. He rose from the chair, regaining the height advantage he had temporarily lost. He was so unnervingly close, as close as a lover. He would barely need to move at all to kiss me.

But he didn't kiss me. He just held my hips and spoke softly into my ear.

'You don't have to do a thing I tell you to, Sarah. You can say no whenever you like. Is that understood?'

I nodded.

'I want you to say yes, though. In fact, I want you to say, "Yes, Sir." Can you say that for me?'

'Yes, Sir.'

He sighed.

'That's perfect. Are you ready?'

'Yes, Sir.'

'You'd better be.'

He let go of me and took a step back, picking up the strop again.

'Well, Sarah, I don't know if this will ever be the same again after the way you've treated it, do you?'

'No, Sir.'

'Exactly what was it you did with it? I want to hear your confession.'

'Oh, God!' *I really don't want to tell you out loud.*

'Understandable, that you should mix me up with a deity, but I'm not your god, Sarah, just your master. Now tell me what you did. I want the truth.'

'I put it somewhere I shouldn't have.'

'And where was that? The airing cupboard?'

'No, Sir.' I probably shouldn't have giggled.

He slapped the leather down on the desk with some force and I jumped.

'So?'

'I, uh, put it next to my, uh, private parts.'

'Your private parts.' He mimicked my prissy voice. 'And once it was there, slap bang up against your private parts, what did you do with it?'

'I, sort of, rubbed it against them.'

'You masturbated with it,' he said, narrowing his eyes in mock horror. 'You committed the sin of self-abuse. With my razor strop.'

'Yes, Sir,' I whispered, shaking with humiliation. Or arousal. Actually, both.

'And what did you think about while you were doing it?'

41

He was too cruel. He knew exactly which buttons to press to rack up the shame and mortification.

'Must I answer that, Sir?'

'Of course.'

'I thought about how it might be used.'

'What, sharpening a razor?'

'No. You know.'

'I don't. Enlighten me.'

'As a thing to, to, hit me with.'

'Oh. As an instrument of punishment, you mean?'

'Yes, Sir.'

'On your hands?'

'No, Sir, not my hands.'

'Where then?'

'Uh.' I put a hand behind me, providing a dumb show I hoped he would pick up on.

'I'm not a fan of mime, Sarah. Say the word.'

'On my ... bottom,' I whispered.

'Oh, I see. That's what you thought about while you were rubbing my razor strop all over your soaking wet cunt, was it? The way it would feel on your bare bottom?'

The word 'cunt' made me quiver with shock, and yet it also made me want to hear it again, in his rich, dark voice, again and again.

'Yes, Sir.'

'Well, now we've arrived at the truth of the matter, I have an idea of what I should do with you.'

'Do you, Sir?'

'Yes, I do. Bend over the desk, Sarah, with your elbows, yes, like so.'

He pushed my spine into position and moved my arms until they were the optimum width apart. I looked down at the green leather I had so often admired, and the gold-leaf pattern that surrounded it.

Jasper Jay, the famous film director, had his palm on my rump, rubbing at the cotton skirt that covered it, assessing its thinness. His other hand lay heavy on my shoulder, holding me down, steadying me. He had placed the strop across my back, resting it there, as a sort of permanent reminder. Was he really going to use it on me?

'Let's see how you take this,' he said, to himself.

He took his hand from my rear and let me experience a moment of pure anticipation before he brought it cracking back down, hard, across my outthrust buttocks.

It forced a breath from me, but not a cry. It was piquant rather than painful, spicy and peppery, moreish. He knew it, so he gave me more, fed my craving, for another dozen strokes, during which I shut my eyes and gave in to the delirious knowledge that I was having my bottom smacked by the internationally fêted Jasper Jay. Lucky old me.

'What do you think of the show so far?' he asked, his hand falling relentlessly.

'Mm hmm,' was all I could think of to say to that. I hoped he interpreted it as blanket approval.

'I'll take it easy this first time,' he said, though I was beginning to gasp. 'But one day, Sarah, when we know each other much better, I promise I'll make you cry.'

One day when we know each other much better. What did he have in mind? I almost pushed myself up, twisted my head towards him, curious to know more.

But he stopped just then and began lifting my skirt, and all other thoughts rushed away, replaced by the imminent display of my pink lace briefs.

His hand pushed the fabric up my thighs, rippling over the protuberant curve and gathering at my waist. Extra warmth, on top of that which he had spanked into my skin, soaked through the lace when he touched it, then he grazed it with his fingernails and the sparks snapped through me.

His hand landed, confusingly, on my bare thigh. I had not expected this and I squeaked and raised my spine a little, but he pushed me right back down.

'Lovely lacy knickers,' he said, covering them with medium-strength strokes. 'I'm going to spank you until this pattern transfers itself to your skin. Won't that be pretty?'

'Yes, Sir,' I moaned, my voice sounding almost the way it did when I came. It was going to be impossible to hide my growing arousal.

'You're already the same colour. Deep pink. Soon you'll be red, though. My favourite shade.'

The heat was increasing, starting to become uncomfortable now. I wondered how long he could go on for before tiring. What if he carried on for an hour or more? What if I asked him to stop and he didn't? He'd said, hadn't he, that I only had to say no. He'd been telling the truth. Yes? Had he? Fuck, I hardly knew him. What kind of idiot was I, making important judgements about people on such a flimsy basis?

'Ouch,' I said experimentally.

He stopped.

I let out a breath.

He yanked down my knickers.

I inhaled again.

'Oh,' I said.

'No?' he murmured, rubbing my stinging bum so very gently. 'Enough?'

'It's OK,' I decided. *I'm telling him it's OK to take down my knickers! Why am I telling him this?* 'Just ... a surprise.'

'Bad girls always get spanked on their bare bottoms, Sarah. I thought you'd know that.'

'Yes, I did. Sorry, Sir.'

'Thank you for your apology. You're deliciously warm now. But not quite the right colour ... so ...'

The crack of his hand making contact with my bare

45

skin was so supercharged with eroticism that I pushed my bottom out for more. I wanted that noise echoing in my ears, ringing around the room. I wanted to make a sound clip of it and listen to it over and over.

He repeated it, with variations, perhaps twenty or thirty times. His hand fell harder and harder, and then he sped up and that was when I started to struggle.

'Painful, is it?' he crooned, dashing off a final half-dozen while he massaged the shoulder he still held me by. 'You should see the glow. Like a glorious sunset.'

He stayed his hand then, using it instead to caress my hot round arse cheeks.

'How was that?' he whispered.

I contemplated my position, bent over a desk with my knickers around my ankles and my soundly spanked bottom on display. I was so wet he must be able to smell me, matching up the aroma with that he'd sniffed on the strop earlier.

Oh. The strop. What about that?

'Thank you, Sir,' I said.

He made a sound of deep satisfaction.

'You're good,' he said. 'You can stay.'

I tried to push myself up but he held me firm.

'Ah, ah, ah, not so fast,' he said.

I heard the slither of leather close to my ear, felt it creep off my back.

'The punishment has to fit the crime, remember.'

46

I thought he might have forgotten. A little sound of dismay leaked from my lips.

'Unluckily for you,' he said, 'you've alighted upon one of the most devastating tools in my box. You'll be feeling the effects of this for a day or so. The leather's so nice and thick, you see, yet it bends to your shape, leaving lovely tight stripes ... but you'll see for yourself. I'm going for ten, since you've never done this before. Count them. If you can't take any more, say "pax". Yes?'

'Yes, Sir.'

'Say it, then, so I know you've been paying attention. What do you say if you've had as much as you can take?'

'Pax, Sir.'

'Right. And you're counting out loud. Right, then. I'm going to hold you down because there's no way you'll stay still for this. Ready. One ... two ... three ...'

'Jesus!' I exclaimed. The stroke was vicious, a scorpion's sting of pure agony. After a ferocious second or so, it burned off, leaving a beautiful throb.

'One, Sir,' I breathed.

That was bad, but was it that bad? I needed another to make sure.

Yes. Yes, it was that bad. The second stroke tore through me, winding me.

'Twooooo, Sir.' I writhed under his hand. He let me wriggle through the pain for a moment or two before pushing down again.

It was horrible, but I wanted another. I wanted to feel overwhelmed, the enormity of submission, the heart-pounding excitement of it. It didn't seem to come without pain. I would just have to get used to it.

But I also wanted to see what he looked like, wielding that thing. I needed a snapshot for my memory bank. I craned my neck, hoping to catch a glimpse.

'Turn around,' he ordered, and he shouted it this time. I hadn't heard him raise his voice until now and it intimidated me. 'Sorry,' he said, after a pause, much more gently. 'I'm sorry. You have to keep still. I don't want to hurt you.'

He chuckled self-consciously.

'Well … you know what I mean. Not really hurt you. Look, you're still OK with this, are you?'

'It hurts a lot. But I don't mind. I want more. I want to know what happens if you give me more.'

'You want to know how the story ends,' he said with an edge of satisfaction.

'Yes.'

'More of a chapter, this,' he ruminated. 'Chapter one. I wonder if it's going to be a slim volume or something along the lines of the Encyclopaedia Britannica. I think we'll have fun finding out anyway. Right. Brace yourself.'

Oh, that burn, that awful, unendurable, shocking burn that forces its heat deep inside me and transforms it into … something else.

'I hate it,' I whimpered. 'Three, Sir.'

I found something inside myself, a core of endurance, or submission, or whatever I wanted to call it – semantics weren't at the forefront of my mind at the time – that took me through the pain and let me embrace it. As a gift or a privilege, because that was how it felt to me.

Jasper was showing me something about myself, giving me an insight into my nature. I learned that I was made for this, made to be thrashed on my bare bottom with an antique razor strop, made to take whatever the higher power had to give.

It made me feel safe.

How paradoxical was that? When it came down to it, the way Jasper treated me, for all its capricious cruelty, made me feel cared for and special. It made me feel love.

When the tenth stroke came, I almost asked for more, even though my thighs were trembling and my bottom felt as if it had been skinned. I had the delusion that I could take as much as he had to give, that I could become one with the pain and make it a part of myself. I know it was some kind of endorphin-related euphoria, but it was powerful and, for that moment, uncontrollable.

'Ten, Sir,' I panted. I hadn't shed a tear, though my eyes stung with sweat. How much would it take to make me cry? One day he would show me.

He stood, his hand still on my shoulder, keeping me immobile while I absorbed the final moments.

'I didn't think you'd make it all the way to ten,' he said.

'I could have taken more,' I said.

He gave my shoulder an affectionate squeeze.

'You're as rare a find as anything in my collection,' he said.

I wondered if he was going to kiss me, or touch me, or do anything to assuage the fire that raged between my legs now that the sting was levelling into a delicious soreness.

He pulled me to my feet and held me against him until I stopped shaking. I squashed my face into his expensive shirt and breathed him in. I could have stayed there for ever, wrapped up and warmed, but eventually he gave my bottom a little pat and whispered, 'Run along now.'

It stung far worse than his razor strop. I jerked my neck back, lips parted in dismay.

'Run along?'

'Yes. We've both got work to do.'

He softened visibly at my appalled expression and stroked my hair.

'Oh, Sarah,' he said. 'Don't get in too deep, my love.'

'I'm not!' Arrogant swine.

'I hope not. Do you want me to fuck you?'

I shook my head, though I did, of course, but it wasn't meant to be like this. It wasn't meant to be this bald, flat question, almost a statement.

'You don't? Well, what's the matter then?'

'I thought … forget it. I was mistaken.'

I tried to wrench myself from his grasp but he held me fast, his eye on me, sizing me up.

'Sarah, you're here for the whole summer. We've got plenty of time. We can get to know each other.'

This was better. I stopped struggling.

'And I want you to want it,' he whispered. 'I want you to want it really badly. I want to make you wait until you can't bear it for another minute. I want to hear you beg me for it.'

He slid his hands under my skirt, which had fallen back down over my bottom, and lifted it again, cupping the sore buttocks, squeezing them.

'I think you're wet,' he said into my ear. 'I think you're a real glutton for punishment, aren't you?'

I tried to remove my ear from the toxic influence of his silken words, but he found it again, and poured more of them in.

'I think I might have to punish you again,' he said. 'Maybe every day. And when you're good and wet and ready, I'll tie your wrists to the bed.' He nipped at my earlobe, so delicately, so devastatingly. 'Then I'll make you spread your legs and hold them wide open for me and do you know what I'll do?'

'No.'

'I'll breathe on your clit. Just one hot breath. And I'll

leave you there, tied up, legs wide, every cell in your body screaming to be fucked. And maybe I'll come back and fuck you later. And maybe I won't.'

He rubbed his nose in my hair, then down my neck.

I almost ground myself against his pelvis. Almost. God, it was hard not to.

Kiss me, I pleaded silently. Kiss my mouth.

But he let go of me, then turned me around by my shoulders and propelled me to the door. I was still hobbled around the ankles by my knickers and I nearly stumbled.

'Take them off,' he said, leaning idly on the desk, watching me. 'And the skirt. Go on.'

I don't know why I obeyed him, but I did, standing before him half-naked, my hands clasped over my pubic triangle.

'Good. You can work like that, can't you? Go on then. And no touching yourself. I'll know if you do.'

His gleaming heartless smile shooed me out of the study and back across the hallway.

I knelt down amongst the Sèvres porcelain, wincing as my strapped bottom touched my heels, and put my face in my hands for a long moment of orientation. I was breathless with lust, longing to touch myself. I had no idea how I was going to get through the rest of this afternoon with my clit swollen like a barrage balloon.

I picked up a vase and stared unseeingly at the painted figures on it, thinking of what had passed, thinking of Jasper and who he might be. What he might be to me.

I couldn't make sense of it, though. The painted figures crystallised, a shepherd and a shepherdess cavorting on a hillside. What a simple life. I envied them.

I picked up my notes and set back to work, my bursts of activity frequently interrupted by an ever-present nag between my thighs and the sore, tight feeling in my bum cheeks.

Was he finding it difficult to work as well? He must have been turned on by it all or why would he have bothered? My nerves stood to attention at a click from his study door and I tried to look extra-busy.

'That'll do for today,' he said, standing in the doorway, watching me. 'I'm going to make dinner. Well, I'm going to order something in anyway. You need to get dressed for it.'

Dressed for dinner? I hadn't brought anything like that with me.

'It's all right,' he said, reading my thoughts. 'I've picked something out for you. I'll leave it on the bed. See you in the dining room at eight sharp.'

He left and I heard his footsteps on the stairs.

I replaced all the porcelain in the cabinets and went over to the window. Just as well nobody could see the house from the road, given my state of partial undress. Looking out at the gardens I thought, for the first time since his departure, of Will.

Where was he tonight?

I stood in the full-length glass arch and imagined Jasper had put me there, as a punishment, while out on the terrace his guests drank tea and ate cucumber sandwiches and played badminton on the lawns beyond. Occasionally they might look over at me and shake their heads, knowing that I was serving my punishment, squinting over for a glimpse of my strapped backside.

I shook the thought from my head before I was tempted to do anything about it. I wasn't allowed to touch myself. Jasper had forbidden it.

This made things even worse, the knowledge of my helpless obedience to his will sending a thrill of pure lust through me.

I had to get to my bedroom while I still could.

Chapter Three

I was avid with curiosity about this outfit he had picked out for me. Was it some kind of ballgown?

On the bed lay a strange little bundle of black lace.

It didn't look like a dress.

I picked it up and held it out. It was some kind of all-in-one body-suit type thing, but with certain parts noticeably missing.

It took a long time to put on, because I kept mistaking armholes for crotch holes and so on, but eventually I prevailed and went to grimace at myself in the full-length mirror. Jesus. I looked utterly whorish.

My legs were the only part of me that were fully covered, in the stretch lace-patterned tights. At least, they were covered to the thigh and then strips of the material linked up with the upper part of the garment in a suspender effect, while the gaps exposed my pussy and my bottom and the sides of my thighs. My waist was nipped in by some cunningly situated embroidery and the plunging cleavage left most of my breasts on display, though my nipples hid behind lace rosettes.

It was a garment whose only function was to make one easily fuckable.

I twirled, noting the deep colour of my bottom, still, parts of it speckled with tiny bruises.

What was he going to do to me now?

Bend me over the table and have me.

My fingers brushed my little thatch of pubic hair, so close to skimming between my lower lips, but I resisted. No touching.

How the hell was I going to eat? I was so strung up with excitement I could barely keep still. I strutted in front of the mirror, running my hands up underneath my hair and pouting like a trademark vamp. I had never seen myself this way before. Was it the way Jasper saw me?

For a moment, I was convinced that all this was some kind of delusional fever dream. Then I looked at the clock, saw that it was nearly eight, and scampered, shoe-less, down to the dining room.

He sat alone at the head of the table. He was dressed to kill in black tie, every hair in place, perfectly composed.

I stopped in the doorframe, wanting to see his reaction to my outrageously rude outfit.

He looked up and smirked, then rose and walked towards me.

His pace was so leisurely, so relaxed that I forgot to feel intimidated. Then he picked up my hand and sniffed my fingertips and the impulse of pleasurable fear kicked back in. He was so unpredictable. Anything could happen.

Having sniffed them, he put my fingers in his mouth, one by one, giving each a sharp little suck.

'Mm,' he said, once this ritual was done. 'You've been a good girl, haven't you?'

I put my damp fingers to my lips, unable to speak, until he encouraged me forward with a hand between my shoulder blades, escorting me to the table.

'Are you always so well behaved?' he asked, pulling out a chair for me.

I sat down. My bare bottom sank into deep velvet pile, easing my residual soreness.

'I'm not a hellraiser, if that's what you're asking.'

He sat down himself, his own seat at the head of the table, at right angles to mine. He had put a serving cloche between us, as if this were a banquet, minus the waiting staff. A bottle of champagne stood in an ice bucket. Both the cloche and the ice bucket were sterling silver and I leaned forward, looking for the hallmark.

57

He seemed to enjoy my scholarly interest, lifting the champagne bottle with a clatter of ice.

'Yes, they're genuine,' he said. 'This bucket's Edwardian. From Tiffany's. You're really into all this, aren't you?'

'Of course. When I was six years old I told my mother I wanted to be one of the experts on Antiques Roadshow.'

'That's cute.' He smiled and poured me a glass of champagne. 'And is that still your ambition?'

'I'm not sure I want to be on TV,' I admitted. I sipped at the champagne, trying to remember the last time I'd had any. When I graduated, possibly. Anyway, I wasn't used to it and the bubbles went up my nose, making me splutter like the sex goddess I'm not. 'I don't think I'm the type.'

'Why not?'

'You have to get your hair done all the time and have spa treatments and, oh, you know, the pressure to look impeccable all the time ...'

'Not on Antiques Roadshow, surely. Besides, you're very attractive.'

'Oh, don't.'

'Don't what? You are. Hasn't anybody ever told you?'

'Only my creepy third-year tutor.'

'What, seriously? What about your boyfriends?'

'No, we weren't ... into that kind of thing. You know, compliments about physical appearance and so forth.'

He furrowed his brow, smiling curiously, and took a sip of his champagne.

'So what were you into?'

'I suppose we liked to think that we were, you know, beyond all that kind of, of frivolity. Shallowness. And that our connection was on a more cerebral level.'

'My God, it sounds like passion incarnate.'

'You're teasing me.'

'Yes, I am. But, Sarah, it sounds drier than the dust on my top-shelf collection of Victorian erotica.'

'Yes, but you work in a world where looks and appearances and visual impressions are all-important. That's not the world for me. It's you people and your film stars that are responsible for so much angst and low confidence and crappy self-esteem. Hardly anyone can look like a movie star – yet we all go crazy trying to do it and feeling like shit if we fail.'

He paused, blinking at me over the rim of his glass.

'That's a fair comment,' he said eventually. 'And an interesting one.'

'Not really. I think it's quite a commonplace point of view.'

'It's your point of view. That's what makes it interesting to me.'

'I'm just a normal person, Jasper.'

'And I'm not.'

He lifted the cloche on a risotto.

'We should eat,' he said.

59

Spooning a pile of sticky rice studded with asparagus on to my plate, he continued the theme.

'So what's normal nowadays, then, Sarah? What are the normal people doing? Tell me all about being normal while you sit there on your sore, spanked arse drinking champagne at my table wearing nothing but a lewd bodystocking.'

That dazzling, cruel smile again. I clamped my thighs together, shamefully aware of the absurdity of my situation.

'Why are you doing this?' I asked quietly.

'Because I want to. And you want me to. Deny it – go on.'

I wanted to, but I couldn't.

'So tell me about your paper-dry boyfriends of yore. Tell me what you did with them.'

'There was only one. He was a student in my year.'

'What was his name?'

'Hugh.'

'And Hugh … I'm trying to picture him now … a university scarf, a bicycle, spectacles.'

'Two out of three,' I said with a grimace. 'No scarf.'

'He was the first then?'

'Yes.'

'I'm jealous of him.'

'No, you aren't.'

'I am. What was he like?'

'Nice.' I couldn't think of another word, which seemed a little damning.

'*Nice?*'

'Nothing wrong with nice.' I shovelled my fork defensively into the rice and took a mouthful.

'I'm nice,' he said, leaning forward on an elbow, smiling his half-demonic half-angelic smile, willing me to react. 'I'm as nice as you want me to be. And in bed – was he nice there too?'

'He was … it's none of your business actually.'

'Oh, that bad, eh?'

My scalp prickled as if I'd been caught thieving. It was true, the sex had been less than stellar. The whole affair had fizzled out after we graduated and picked different universities for our PhD studies.

'It's good that you finished it, then,' Jasper opined, turning his attention to the food.

'Who said I finished it? It was mutual, in the end. It just ended. We still email, you know, as friends.'

'How very fucking civilised.'

'Yes, it is. You're kind of an arsehole, you know? Just for your information. At least, that's how you're coming across. I don't know if you're aware of it.'

He stared, eyebrows up, until I didn't think I'd ever be able to swallow the mouthful of risotto I was shifting from cheek to cheek.

'Thank you for your honesty,' he said at last.

'I thought you'd like to know. Why are you trying to belittle me and my past and my life choices? What do you think I'm going to take from that, apart from an impression that you're a bit of a git?'

'I've always found that submissives like a bit of theatrical arrogance.'

'Submissives? What, like, a homogeneous ball of girls who like being spanked?'

He sat back and looked me over, his gaze roaming all over me, ending at my ridiculously plunging cleavage.

'You're right,' he said. 'I'm just not a very nice person. Perhaps I'm even a bad person. But I'm a good master. And I can show you things. I want to show you so many things, Sarah. If you'll let me.'

Every ounce of common sense screamed at me to run. But I was trapped, enticed by the beguiling promise of sinful pleasure to come. He had a hold on me. It just wouldn't do to let him know.

'I'll consider it,' I said.

'Good. Well, let's finish eating, shall we?'

I dug into the risotto, but my appetite wasn't much in evidence, having been replaced by a tugging tension in my lower abdomen.

This was not alleviated by the sudden arrival of Jasper's shoe against my foot, then my ankle, then sliding up my calf. I chewed doggedly on a stalk of asparagus but it seemed more and more probable that his footwear journey was going to end at my open crotch.

I put my fork down and shot him a panicked glance.

He winked at me and moved his foot higher, shoving it in between my thighs, parting them. He had to stretch a little and shift forward in his seat but he managed to get his toecap right inside my pussy lips and he held it there, swivelling it this way and that, for about ten seconds while I sat and stared at the ice bucket.

Then he took it away again and said, 'Strawberries. Come here.'

I hesitated and he pushed back his chair and held out his hand.

'Come on, Sarah. I'm going to give you your dessert.'

'My just dessert?'

'Yes. Exactly.'

He put me on the edge of the table in front of him, my bottom on his place mat. Once he had moved all the silverware and plates out of the way, he had me lie down with my legs dangling off the edge of the table, following the fall of the fine white cloth, almost to the floor.

Once I lay in my place, looking up at the chandelier and the plaster ceiling rose, he stood between my knees and leaned over me to reach for a dish of strawberries. He took one, dipped it in cream, and put it to my lips. Some dim remembrance of being told never to eat in this position lurked at the fringes of my mind, but the cream was slick and the fruit smelled full and ripe and I opened my mouth for it.

Jasper wiped it along my lips until they were coated

in cream, then he pushed it towards my teeth, crushing it there until I took a bite.

'Mmm,' he said, his face low over mine. I could feel the lump of his erection, inside his dress trousers, pressing into my exposed pussy. 'Is that sweet?'

'Mmm,' I replied in kind, sucking on the pink flesh.

'Let me taste,' he whispered and he dropped still lower and his mouth clamped down on mind so that we both licked at the strawberry simultaneously, its mushed pulp spread by our tongues into the far corners.

He repeated this with a number of soft fruits, plunging us again and again into this messy, juicy, creamy version of a kiss until I felt utterly abandoned to sensuality. I twitched my groin against his, rubbing my pussy up and down his trouser-covered bulge, taking his tongue deep inside my throat, pushing back into his mouth with mine.

'You've had yours,' he murmured, pushing the last remnants of a strawberry on to my tongue and lifting his head a little. 'Now I want mine.'

I don't know what I hoped he meant by this, but he could have meant anything at all and I'd have consented to it like a shot. My body wanted him to do things to it that it had never heard of, my mind having conveniently located its off-switch at some point during the preceding events.

He picked up a fistful of strawberries and stood up, spreading my thighs wide with his free hand.

'There are rules for this game,' he told me. I watched his fingers close around the fat red fruits, mashing them a little, pink juice dribbling on to his skin. I wanted to lick it off him. 'I'm going to eat these off of you. You're going to like it, I promise you. You're going to like it a lot. But you aren't going to come. Because I don't want you to, not yet. Let's see how you do with that, shall we?'

Without further explanation, he pasted the oozing strawberries into my lower lips, some of them shoved up inside me, others pressed between his palm and my clit. He pushed and smashed and rubbed them to pulp, then he dropped to his knees and began to feast.

I raised my neck, helpless and half-aghast, half-enraptured by his move.

I saw his head of dark hair and his eyelids, lowered, the lashes fluttering as he licked and lapped and sucked me all over. My clit was bigger and fatter than any strawberry, slipping wantonly into his mouth, begging for his hot breath and his wicked tongue. But it was wrong of it to beg, because I had to somehow rise above this riot of erotic sensation and batten down the initial stirrings of climax.

How was this even going to be possible?

He pushed his tongue up inside me, swirling it around to catch every last trace of the mingled juices – strawberries and sex. He smacked his lips and moaned with arousal and devoured me as if I were the proverbial manna in the desert.

And that's what he seemed like to me, in that instant. Manna in my desert.

He held my lips apart with his thumbs and moved in even deeper. I was not going to be able to hold out … I could feel a treacherous little flutter somewhere at the base of my bum cheeks, spiralling back and joining up with my cunt. Everything began to connect in a terrible, unstoppable game of join-the-dots, coming together with alarming magnitude. I was not going to be able to stop it. I had to stop it. I couldn't stop it.

'Oh dear,' he said, long and low, once I'd spilled my strawberry orgasm into his mouth. He took some time to relish the flavour of my undoing, rolling his tongue around his cheeks, smacking his lips. His thumbs retained their positions on my labia.

'I tried not to.'

'I know,' he said, and he released my pussy lips, bent over me and kissed me for such a long time that I thought I might drown in the sensual, berry-scented lusciousness of it. 'It's an acquired skill,' he said, pulling me up by my fingers. 'And you're going to acquire it. Though I don't think it'll be easy for you.'

'Don't you? Why not?'

'Because you're a very responsive little bunny, aren't you?' He tangled his fingers in my hair and pulled it,

66

making me fall into his kiss again. 'You want it pretty badly, hmm?'

I felt hot and prickly and ashamed at my obvious readable lustfulness. He knew I would spread my legs for him at the drop of an antique gag. It was entirely possible that he could make me come just by looking at me. I was annoyingly transparent, and powerless in the face of his perception.

'Don't worry, Sarah,' he whispered into my ear. 'I'm going to train you well.'

He sat back down in his chair, leaving me leaning my bare bottom on the edge of the table, and smiled at me.

'What a mess,' he said. 'I'll have to have that tablecloth laundered. And as for my shirt ...' He frowned down at the pink-splodged cotton. 'Tell you what. Why don't you go and grab a shower and come back down to the drawing room?'

'Oh, OK.' A shower sounded good. I almost thanked him, then caught myself. What did I have to thank him for? If I wanted to take a shower, I was free to take a shower. He wasn't my drill sergeant, for pity's sake.

I was obviously falling deeper into the submissive mindset, I thought with an impulse of fear. Perhaps I should try to check my descent, just a little, even if it might mean missing out on what promised to be the most mind-blowing sex imaginable.

As I arrived at the door, he stopped me.

'Oh, Sarah.'

I turned.

'Yes?'

'When you come back down,' he said, 'I want you naked.'

He had changed his shirt by the time I came back down to the drawing room, but he still wore the black dress trousers and the shinier-than-shiny shoes. His clean shirt was more relaxed, open at the neck, exposing his Adam's apple and a patch of chest, tan and sparsely scattered with hair.

He sat by the fireplace, accessorising nicely with the black cast-iron mouldings of the surround. I didn't think my pale, unclothed skin would blend quite so well.

I don't know why I found the nakedness so challenging. He had, after all, caught me in post-coital disarray at our first meeting, and the bodystocking had hardly provided a decent level of coverage. It felt awkward and unnatural to be completely bare, though, and I could not for a moment forget the fact that every part of me was vulnerable and on show to him.

Instinctively, I put my hands over my pubic triangle, protecting my breasts with my upper arms.

He shook his head.

'Move your hands,' he said. 'Are you embarrassed?'

'A bit.' I pouted for a moment then clenched my fists at my side.

'I like embarrassment. It suits you. Your little rosy cheeks. Come over here.'

I stalked forward and stood, hunched and shivering a little, in front of him.

'Get that footstool and bring it here.'

I picked it up – rosewood with dark-green velvet upholstery, elegant carving on the legs – and set it down by his chair.

'Right. Now kneel on it. But spread your legs wider … that's it.'

I felt like an exhibit and I couldn't face him. What should I do with my hands? They hung there uselessly while I endured the unforgiving laser of his attention.

'I need you to look at me, Sarah.'

I did as he told me, but kept my eyelids low. My whole face twitched with the effort of not looking away.

'I told you earlier not to come while I was licking that juicy little cunt of yours, didn't I? But you came anyway. Right?'

'Yeah.'

'What's that you say?' He cupped a hand behind his ear, his voice suddenly hard-edged.

'Yes, Sir.' The words came as easily as breathing, surprising me. I was meant to say them.

'Why did you do that?'

'I couldn't help myself.' I paused and waited for it to say itself. 'Sir.'

69

'Right. And why couldn't you help yourself?'

'Because what you were doing to me … it was very … it made me … lose control.'

He smiled but his eyes were flints.

'I made you lose control? Well, then, if you can't control yourself, you're going to need me to do it for you. Aren't you?'

'Yes, Sir.'

'I can do that.'

'I know you can.'

He raised the leg that was crossed over the other, waving his polished shoe in the air beneath my nose.

'Look at my shoe, Sarah. It's got a kind of white patch on it. Do you know what that is?'

Yes, I knew what that was. I swallowed guiltily, remembering how he had played footsie with my pussy under the table.

'Yes, Sir.'

He waited for me to elaborate.

'It's, er, from me. When I was wet.'

'When you were wet. You were very wet, weren't you?'

'Yes, Sir.'

'Are you wet now?'

'I … don't know.' I did know. I was soaking.

'I don't tolerate lying, you know, Sarah. But I'll give you another chance. Are you wet now?'

I heaved the words out. 'I think so, Sir.'

'You'd better make sure.'

I blinked.

He raised his eyebrows and nodded downwards.

'Yes. You know what to do. Go on.'

I flapped for a second before touching my fingertip, as quickly and lightly as I could, to my vagina.

'Well? Show me.'

I held out my hand, the finger pointing upwards. He took me by the wrist, bent forward and sniffed.

'You are,' he said. 'That's good. We can move on to the next stage.'

'Oh. Can we, Sir?'

'Yes. Open your lips and show me your clit. I want to see it.'

I couldn't help a sigh and a grimace.

'Another thing you're going to have to learn, Sarah, is a quick and graceful response to my commands. I think we'll try that next.'

I leaned back on my calves, trying to angle my pussy towards his view, and splayed the lips with my fingers. He leaned forward, frowning over his inspection, which seemed to last a long time.

'You're definitely ready,' he diagnosed. 'Why are you wet again, Sarah? I haven't touched you. Is it because you're naked?'

'Partly, I think. And just ... you. Being you. The way you are.'

'The way I am?'

'So ... confident. And, like, just assuming that I'm going to do as you say. I imagined doms to be ... shoutier. And like, you know, you smile a lot. I didn't think they smiled. For some reason. Not sure why.'

'Everyone's different, Sarah. That's humanity for you.'

'I know. I feel a bit stupid, actually, but that stereotype had popped up in my fantasy life for so long, it became a kind of dom avatar.'

He nodded sagely.

'So we've established that you find me incredibly sexy. This is worth knowing.'

I smirked at him, half-annoyed, all-attracted.

Without warning, he pushed his toecap between my thighs again and rubbed his shoe in my juices. The cold, smooth leather on my clit made me let out a tiny moan. I tried to get it away, but he shook his head.

'Keep it there,' he said. 'Hold on to my leg if you need to. You're going to masturbate on my shoe, Sarah, and when you can feel your orgasm coming, you're going to tell me.'

'I can't do that!' I said aghast.

'You can. You're going to. Look, you've already started.'

He was right. I'd gripped his calf and was rocking along in rhythm with his slow rotations from the ankle. My thighs flexed and relaxed, my bottom pumping in small but agitated motions, while I painted the leather with my streaming juices.

My breasts swung to and fro and I stared down at the dark cloth of Jasper's trousers while he issued periodic words of encouragement.

'Faster than that, Sarah. Really get stuck in. Feel it building up. You want it.'

I felt dirty and sordid, disgusted with myself, bringing myself off on a man's shoe, but my arousal fed on those feelings and flowered all the more.

'Touch your nipples,' he said.

I let go of his leg with one hand and obeyed without question, stroking them mindlessly while the room faded out and became one giant dark mass of erotic concentration.

'Look at you. One, two, hump my shoe. What a gorgeous little slut you are.'

I opened one eye. The word 'slut' had sounded oddly soft, an endearment, not an insult. His expression backed my perception up; his pupils were giant in his eyes.

'Do you like it when I call you a slut, Sarah? Some girls don't. If you don't like it, I won't say it.'

''S OK,' I panted.

'Good. Slutty little piece, rubbing her pussy all over my bloody expensive shoe ... are you nearly there yet?'

'Nearly ... nearly ...'

I dug my fingers into his calf. It was coming. I had to tell him, but if I told him … No, I had to tell him.

'I'm going to come,' I wailed, and he yanked his foot away so hard and fast that I almost fell off the stool, having to steady myself by lunging for his knee.

The first little spasms of climax flickered uselessly and then died, denied their moment. I wanted to order him to put his foot back, now.

'Poor Sarah,' he crooned. 'She wanted it but she couldn't have it. Take a few deep breaths, girl, and I'll put it back there.'

I inhaled all the air in the room, levelling my head. Then his foot was back between my legs, taking all my frustrated lust up a notch, holding it there, keeping me on the brink with the slow teasing of my clit until I seized him and bucked on his shoe with my teeth gritted and my hair flying everywhere.

'Don't you dare come,' he said, and I held myself still.

I can't believe I held myself still. I was so close, and I'd spoiled my own orgasm again. But I wanted to please him, very much, and that seemed more important than my moment of fleeting pleasure.

'Good girl,' he said. He gave my clit one last prod and took his foot away. 'That was good. Come and sit with me.'

I hoped that might be a euphemism for 'come and have wild sex with me'.

74

I shambled forwards into his waiting arms and curled up on his lap, my head on his shoulder, my thigh pressing into one almighty erection.

He tilted my chin for a kiss, holding the back of my neck while he played on my unsatisfied, pulsing desire. He kissed with unbearable depth and sensuality while my poor pussy begged for some attention.

'Do you want to come?' he whispered.

I nodded, burying my face in his neck.

He reached out to the occasional table beside him, on which stood a chinoiserie casket, and plucked out a cellophane square.

Oh, a condom. Everything clenched with excitement. We were going to fuck after all.

He unbuckled his belt, then moved my hand to his crotch, wordlessly instructing me to continue while he dealt with the wrapper.

I worked at the buttons, my face aflame, my eyes directed downward, not daring to look up in case he saw the full force of my desire for him.

'You understand, Sarah, that if you are my lover, you have to be mine alone?'

I wrenched the fly apart and tried to ease the trousers over Jasper's behind, with his assistance.

'That's fine,' I muttered.

'No more Will,' he elucidated.

'Oh. God. No.' I'd forgotten all about him. My greedy

fingers reached for the waistband of his boxers. Silk. It was warm from him.

'I don't share,' he said. 'Not unless I'm in the mood.'

My eyelids flickered upwards, checking his face for signs of casual humour. There weren't any. He was absolutely focused on me, eyes signalling his intent better than the finger and thumb fidgeting with the condom.

I unveiled his cock. I'd like to say I did it with a flourish, but it was more a guilty, furtive kind of motion. As soon as I saw it, I had this mad craving to bend and kiss it.

He helped me remove the trousers and underwear from shot, leaving them somewhere in the region of his ankles, then he slid the condom over his erection. No kisses yet, or, at least, not of that nature. He pulled me astride him and caught my lips with his, holding me tightly by the shoulders until he broke off.

'You need to come, don't you?' he whispered. Feathery fingers drifted down my spine, then the hand they belonged to stroked my still warm bottom.

'Yes, Sir.'

'I think you deserve a little treat,' he said. 'But not until I say so.'

I could only blink, uncertain what he might mean by this.

He nudged at my hip, gently directing me towards the tip of his cock. I tried to lower myself, but he held me just a whisker above it, so near, yet so far.

'What I mean is that you have to ask me for your orgasm, love. No, not ask. Ask isn't right. Beg for it.'

He smiled, playfully wicked, nuzzling my hair.

'And you wait for my permission. Can you do that?'

'I'm ... not sure.'

'Can you try for me?'

'Yes, Sir.'

He let me circle his cock head with my pussy, occasionally rubbing at the very tip.

'Good. Now, how much do you want it?'

'Oh, a lot. Please let me have it.'

'Have what?'

'Your cock, Sir.'

'Beautifully spoken.'

The words had sounded rough and foreign to me, but his opinion made my scalp tingle with pride.

He let me take the first inch of him inside me. I could feel how slick and wet I was but even so I was highly conscious of how his initial foray stretched me wide. I gasped with the sudden invasion and felt myself strain.

'You're feeling that, hmm?' He kissed my forehead, rubbed his nose against mine.

'Oh ... yes.'

'I'm trying to take this slowly but I just want more of you. You're tight ... no, it's no use. I can't wait.'

He loosened his grip on my hips and let me rock my way down his hard shaft, taking him in by delicious increments, feeling every captivated moment of my penetration.

'You can't wait either, eh?' My enthusiasm was difficult to mask and he crooned, 'Ohhhh yes,' as I sank still further.

I reached a point beyond which it didn't seem possible to take any more and tightened my muscles nervously.

'It's OK,' he said, patting my bottom. 'It's all in. All the way. How does it feel?'

'So full,' I whispered. 'I can't believe I took it all.'

'Oh, you know all the right things to say,' he said with a little darting kiss. 'Are you sure you haven't done this before?'

I shook my head and laid it on his shoulder, overwhelmed with the position I found myself in. How had I arrived here, on the end of this man's cock, ready to beg him for my release?

'So, what are you waiting for?' he said. 'Show me how you grind those hips.'

I was painfully aware that I had been hovering on the tip of orgasm for a long time already. I would have to take this quite slowly and try to fix my mind on his pleasure. The closer I could get him to his orgasm, the more kindly disposed he would be towards granting mine. At least, it seemed a sensible equation.

So I made a study of the feel of his cock in me and the reactions each little move I made brought from him.

He liked me to rock forward until my breasts were almost in his face, presented for his delectation, and he also liked me to straighten my spine and jolt and pant like a rodeo cowgirl. He liked to hold me by the elbows and restrict my movements when I broke the speed limit, shaking his head, warning me not to rush.

'I'm enjoying this too much,' he said. 'Let's make it last.'

Oh, but I didn't want to hear those words. I wanted to come. I could feel my climax bubbling underneath, rising with every tiny spark of friction.

I tried all the nefarious means I could. I sucked at his nipples. I licked beneath his earlobe. I kissed him like a drunken fool, all tongues and biting until he smacked my bum and made me stop.

'You only have to ask,' he reminded me.

But I didn't want to ask! I wanted him to come, then I could just follow along in his wake, surfing the remains of his wave.

'I'm asking now,' I wailed. Dear God. It was so close. I was going to start coming mid-sentence.

'Nicely,' he insisted, pushing four fingers into the furrow of my arse.

Why did he have to do that? The gesture, of such implicit ownership, threw me into a madness of sensation.

'Please, Sir, may I come?' I gibbered.

'I'm going to have to say yes, aren't I?' he sighed, and he was, because I was already there.

'Uh huh,' I said, or an approximation thereof.

'Yes, go on, then.' He tutted and rolled his eyes, but there was humour behind it all, and fond indulgence.

At last I could give myself over to the shooting sparks that heralded my orgasm. No more cruel ruination. I immersed myself in the centrifugal rush, the spread and reach of it, roaring in my ears, taking me into its vortex.

'Thank me for it,' he said, seemingly from some distance away.

'Thank you, Sir,' I said, through the aftershocks.

'Right. Now hold on tight.'

He stood up, then, with me still attached, and lowered me on to the hearthrug. I wrapped my legs around his back and lay, floating happily, while he thrust away, good, hard strokes that almost built me up to another peak. But not quite, because he grabbed my wrists and pinned them over my head before his face contorted and his panting jerked all over the place. That moment of blissful helplessness touched me more than I could say; so uncharacteristic of him, and yet so telling. Underneath the effortlessly dominant veneer, he needed the love, needed the validation, just like everyone else.

'Your face,' he said, minutes later, lying beside me. 'You have the best range of expressions when you're being fucked. I'd love to film you.'

'Oh, God, no,' I said instinctively. I'd always been camera-shy. Everything-shy, if I'm honest.

'Why not?'

'You're a professional filmmaker. You wouldn't be able to resist showing it to somebody.'

He raised his eyebrows, as if disappointed in my low opinion of him, then he seemed to accept it.

'You're probably right,' he said. 'I'm a big show-off. Or, the term I prefer, an artist.'

I smiled. 'An auteur,' I said.

'That's right.' He tweaked my nose. 'Or are you teasing me? I hope you're not teasing me.'

'I wouldn't dare.'

'I should think not. What if I promised, solemnly and faithfully, not to show anyone?'

'It would still exist. And, some day in the future, somebody would find it in your archive and it would be exhibited as a lost treasure. Jasper Jay's secret porn stash.'

He chuckled and kissed me.

'So what? We'd both be long gone. Why not brighten up somebody's drab future with a moment of joy, captured for all time?'

'You're very persuasive.'

'I know.'

We both stared up at the light patterns on the ceiling for a few moments.

'So can I persuade you into my bed?' he asked, yawning.

'I think you just did.'

81

Chapter Four

The morning was a strange time of half-light, sleeping and fucking, the swish of rain falling into the lush lawns outside. By the time the rain stopped, Jasper and I knew a great deal about each other's bodies, and my cunt had been fully acquainted with his cock on three further occasions.

After the last time, he went down to the kitchen to get coffee. I lay on my stomach and drowsed until he came back, sat beside me on the bed and ran his hand over my bottom.

'Bruises,' he said. 'I shouldn't have started you with the strop. It's too heavy for a novice.'

I snorted at the word 'novice', thinking of nuns.

'It doesn't hurt,' I said, and it didn't particularly, even

when he pushed down with his thumb. I was more concerned about the fiery sting in my pussy.

'Doesn't it? Damn. Losing my touch. Sit up then, and have some coffee.'

I rolled over and shifted to a sitting position. Actually, when I'd said it didn't hurt ... it did. A little bit. I liked the pain, though, and would have felt disappointed with a full and swift recovery. I needed the reminder, the proof that it had actually happened. I felt wild with sensuality, as if the more he took from me, the more I had to give.

He looked pale and tired but endlessly, ridiculously desirable to me. He smiled that open-mouthed, insolent, almost-sneer of a smile, and I was wet again, instantly. I gripped the handle of my coffee mug until it wore a groove into my finger and tried to keep my breathing even.

'So how does this work?' I asked.

'How does what work?'

'You and me. Us. Here.'

'How do you want it to work?'

'Is it up to me?'

'Of course.'

I was stumped for a moment. How could it be up to me?

'I mean ... this is real? Is it?'

He reached over and pinched me, quite hard.

'You're not dreaming,' he said.

'Ouch! I didn't think I was. I mean ... this is a thing. You and me. A ...'

'Relationship?'

'Not a one-night stand?'

'Do you want it to be?'

Oh God, stop asking me what I want!

'No. I mean, no. I want ... more.'

'Good. So do I.'

'But ...' I paused to sip delicately at my coffee. 'I'm not sure how it works.'

'So you said. Well, Sarah, I'll try and help you.' He leaned closer to me, whispering into my ear. 'You see, in nature, there are two sexes, one is male – that's me – and one is female – that's you ...'

'Oh, stop it.' I jogged his elbow and he almost spilled his coffee, which, I gathered from his frown, would have landed me in a whole heap of trouble. 'Sorry. I mean, this whole, uh, kinky thing. How does it work? Am I, like, your servant at your beck and call all day long? Or ... not?'

'Oh, Sarah.' He raised his eyes to heaven and slid his free arm around my shoulder. 'There are no rules. There is no one way to have a D/s relationship.'

'D/s?'

'Dominant and submissive. You tailor it to your own needs. Whatever you want it to be, it can be, as long as both parties are in agreement. So, the real question is, what do you want it to be?'

84

'I don't know enough about it.'

He shrugged. 'That's a fair point. You're one of those people who needs to know everything about everything, aren't you?'

I blushed. 'Guilty as charged.'

'Well, rather than spend a month trawling the internet for all the information that's out there – most of it conflicting – why don't you just go with the flow? Do you want me to take the lead?'

'Well, yeah. I can't. Besides, isn't that the whole point?'

'It's the role I play. But you write the script, essentially. You make the cuts. Anything you don't want in there is out. You're the Lord Chamberlain and his censors.'

I laughed. 'So I have ultimate power over your production?'

'You could put it like that.'

'So, with this, then – with us – can I just do what you say? And if I don't like what you say …'

'Say no? Sure. But sometimes saying no is part of the game. I feel that this is especially so with you, because sometimes it's hard for you to admit what you want. So instead of saying no, you can use the safeword. Do you remember the safeword?'

'Pax,' I said.

'Ten out of ten.'

I glowed.

'You like that, don't you?' he said. 'You like getting

the answers right. You like getting full marks on your tests. I think I'll have to work with that tendency ... we could have some interesting scenes.'

I drank the dregs of my coffee.

'Aren't you going back to France?'

'Not for six weeks.'

'Six weeks. And you're going to be here all that time?'

'Yes. I've got things I can work on. I might have to go to the odd meeting or ceremony or ...' He sighed. 'I owe myself a break. I've worked flat-out for the last three years. I need some quiet time to empty my head, make some space for new project ideas.'

'A holiday.'

'A retreat.' He held up his hand, forbidding my further utterance. 'Do you hear that?' he whispered.

I couldn't hear anything. Even the rain had stopped. I shook my head.

'That's what I mean. Silence. I never hear it. There's always a ringing phone or traffic outside or cheering or oceans of flattery or ...' He sighed. 'I forget how much I like silence.'

I took a breath, about to speak, but he cut over me.

'So you aren't speaking today,' he said. 'Not a word, until I say so. Well, except that one word. You're allowed that. Do you understand? Nod for yes.'

I nodded, my face burning. I hoped this wasn't a comment on my conversational skills. Did he find me inane? Tedious? Stupid? I tried to banish my insecurities, but he must have seen an element of them.

'It won't be easy for me either,' he said. 'I like talking to you. You have a fresh take on things. But just for today ... silence. Now, go and shower.'

I presented myself for breakfast in the kitchen in my usual long skirt and top-and-scarf combo. He stopped me before I sat down and asked me to show him my underwear.

I almost asked why, but checked myself in time. Instead, I silently pulled up my top and then lifted my skirt, my pulse racing. Despite the soreness below, I felt ready to take more of him, tingling with the shameful joy of submission.

'Too much,' he said. 'Go upstairs and take it off. You aren't going to need underwear for the next six weeks. Unless I ask you to wear it. Go on, then.' He waved the spatula at me. I could imagine that being quite a useful spanking implement.

When I came back down, he beckoned me over to the counter, where he was buttering toast. With his other hand, he felt my breasts through the thin cotton top, rubbing at my nipples until they stood out through the fabric, bullet-hard and unmistakable. When that was done to his satisfaction, he lifted my skirt and checked for the presence of knickers. Finding none, he rewarded me with a luscious, filthy, grope-filled snog.

'Sit down,' he said, sliding eggs on to the toast before sorting out more coffee. 'But you have to raise your skirt. I want your bare bottom touching the seat. And you can lift up your top too. And keep your legs wide apart.'

Sitting like that, with my top bunched over the top of my breasts and my thighs split while the varnished wooden seat chilled my bare bum, I couldn't escape the reality of my submission. It was profound and absolute, and it was going to touch every aspect of my daily life.

Jasper watched me, smiling slyly, as he dug into his breakfast. I could barely touch mine, my appetite killed by the overwhelming presence of sex in the air around me, touching my skin, feeding itself into me.

'Eat up,' he said, pointing at my plate with his knife. 'You need it, girl. I've plans for you.'

It was an order. I had to obey.

I made a decent attempt at eating my eggs, but the toast stuck in my throat. The coffee didn't help, so strong it gave me jitters. I spilled a drop and it landed on my nipple, making me gasp and almost make a sound. But I managed not to.

Jasper tutted and dabbed my nipple with some kitchen roll, for much longer than was strictly necessary. Then he kissed it better.

Dropping down between my knees, he had a good long look at my widespread pussy, prodding at it until I winced.

'That's a well-fucked pussy,' he diagnosed. 'Swollen and red, it is. I think we'll have to take it a bit easy today. But there are lots of things we can do that don't involve the old in-out. Aren't there?'

He raised flashing eyes to me.

I bit my lip and made a gesture intended to convey the phrase 'You tell me.'

He smiled. 'So much to learn.'

As it happened, I didn't learn much that day beyond the fact that I could fall asleep on my knees, polishing silver. My energetic induction into the possibilities of BDSM had exhausted me and I spent most of the day in bed – my bed in my room, while Jasper glided about below almost noiselessly. It was like being alone in the house.

The day after that, though, waking refreshed and with the bruises on my bottom fading rapidly, I knew I would not be getting off so lightly.

I presented myself in the kitchen for breakfast wearing a longish dress and nothing else. He had said the day before that he preferred shoes to be taken off in the house, to preserve the floors, and it was too hot for hosiery, so my bare feet crossed the cold stone flags to the table, toes curling up with each step.

'Good morning, Sleeping Beauty,' he said. He was leaning against the counter, eating a bowl of cereal. 'I can't be bothered cooking this morning. Get yourself whatever you want.'

'Oh. Right.' I had rather enjoyed being cooked for by him, but I busied myself with the toaster and poured myself a cup of tea from the pot.

'Sun's out,' he remarked, and it was true that the kitchen was flooded with early-morning light, birdsong filtering through the open window.

'Summer's come,' I agreed.

'Good day for a picnic.'

'Is it?' I gave him a swift glance. He wore the expression of a man who was making plans.

'I'd say so. Right.' He put the empty bowl in the sink. 'You sort yourself out. I'm going for a run, then I need to get a few things in town. I want you to meet me, in three hours' time, by the lake in the grounds.'

And he was off.

I found it a little disorientating that he was perfectly normal one minute and benignly dictatorial the next. There had been nothing perverse in our breakfast conversation, and yet the whole exchange seemed to carry such a powerful undercurrent that it felt intensely sexual. Perhaps it was just the effect he had on me.

I got on with my tea and toast and wondered about the day ahead.

The sun grew hotter and fiercer and I was glad not to be wearing any underwear when I set out through the grounds to the lake. I had not put any shoes on either and the grass was blissfully cool and gentle on my bare feet.

Every moment of my journey bore a burden of sensuality – the warmth on my skin, the heavy scents of summer in bloom, the quality of light through the verdant surroundings. And I was walking to meet my master. My destination was sex.

My light cotton dress swished around my thighs. I already knew that I was wet between them, my clit hanging heavy, as if it knew what lay in store. If I looked downwards, I could see my nipples dinting the floral-patterned fabric. I hoped this would please him.

To reach the lake, I had to pass through a small wooded area. My skin chilled in the dappled shade, and I hugged my arms around myself. The sounds were different in here, closer and more intense, and there was a hissing.

No.

That wasn't just the rustle of leaves. It was a person.

'Psst! Sarah!'

I swung around to see Will peering out from behind a tree.

'Christ, Will. You scared me to death. What are you doing?'

'What are you doing, more to the point. He didn't fire you then?'

'No.' I felt heat suffuse my cheeks. Was it going to be obvious to him that Jasper and I were lovers now?

'Oh my God, he's shagging you.'

Apparently it was.

'Will …'

'He is, isn't he? The dirty sod. Are you into all that, then? All his kinky games?'

'Will, shut up. Why are you here?'

'I've come to see you. But obviously you aren't interested, now you've got hot-shot film director into bed.'

'It's not like that.'

'What is it like then?'

I gazed into his bullish, hostile face and wondered what I ever saw in him, beyond a salve for my loneliness. He was good-looking enough but he was boring underneath, and unimaginative. It wasn't as if we'd been consumed with deathless passion, was it? It was just pointless, time-filling sex. Why did he feel he had this claim on me?

'It's none of your business,' I said. 'Jasper and I … we like each other. That's all.'

'God, listen to her. "Jasper and I". You sound like the Queen.'

'Look, you have to go. I'm meeting him. He's at the lake. If he sees you here …'

'I can't believe you'd just dump me like this. For him! After what he did to me.'

'I'm sorry he sacked you, but …' I raised my hands in supplication. There was really nothing more to be said.

'Yeah, sorry, are you? Right. Well, you might not be now, but you will be. Both of you.'

92

'Oh, stop making vague threats and bugger off. Or I will go and tell Jasper you're here, and I don't think you'd want that.'

'Oh, lovely,' he said, bearing down on me, his eyes so tight and mean. 'What a charmer. I know how to pick 'em, don't I? Never mind, Sarah, Jasper can do what he wants with you. I hope it's painful. I'm sure it will be. Fuck you.'

I had taken several steps backwards in alarm, but he didn't try to touch me, simply stormed off through the undergrowth with a tremendous rustle and crackle.

I stood for a moment, stalled by dismay, all my joyful, lustful anticipation of the day's delights forgotten.

Should I do something about this? Tell Jasper?

But I decided against it. I didn't want anything to overshadow our picnic, and Will was just an unwelcome intruder from real life who had gone and would not be back. I stepped out of the shade, into the sun, back into my fantasy-made-flesh.

From the top of the slope I could see Jasper, sitting on a picnic blanket in a white linen shirt and light trousers, reading a book. A basket stood beside him.

I took some time to just look at him, let the sight of him fill me up, colouring in that greyness of spirit Will had left behind. I took a deep breath and began to walk down.

He looked up and put his book aside. His teeth shone

brighter than the sun, glinting below his sunglasses. He must have them professionally whitened, I thought.

'You're a little bit late,' he greeted me, patting the rug beside him.

I sat down, feeling suddenly guilty about the Will encounter.

'Am I? Sorry. I thought I left the house in plenty of time. What are you reading?'

'Don't change the subject.' He dropped the book into the picnic basket and wagged a finger at me. 'We are discussing your punctuality.'

'Oh, dear. Are we?' I tried to look appealing and penitent.

'Yes, we are. And after discussing it, we are addressing it.'

'So I'm in trouble?'

'The best kind of trouble.' He smiled and the little edge of fear I'd been nursing fell away. He was such a good actor; it made all the role-play rather too realistic sometimes. 'First, you need to take off your dress.'

'Really?'

His only answer to that was a hard stare.

I took off the dress, baring myself to the lakeland wildlife. And ... I looked swiftly back to the woodland. Had Will really gone? What if he was still there, watching us? He would see me sitting naked next to the fully clothed Jasper. The thought lent a strange urgency to my arousal. I straightened my spine and pushed back my shoulders, wanting Jasper to know that I was doing my best to look good for him.

'Good,' he said. 'But the sun's pretty ferocious today. You'll need some lotion.'

He took a bottle of factor 30 sunblock from the basket, poured some into his palm and began slathering it over me, starting with my breasts.

I sat, patient and still, while he massaged the pale unguent all over me, with special attention to my nipples.

'Don't want sunburnt nipples, do we?' he said, when my breath began to shorten, my body screaming for him to just jump on and take me.

'No,' I breathed.

'That would be quite terrible.' He rolled them gently between finger and thumb, making the most of their slipperiness. I smelled of holidays and it made me reckless.

'I want you,' I said.

He smiled, but made no reply, simply increasing the pressure on my poor nipples until I gasped.

He had me turn around and kneel with my elbows on the blanket while he attended to my shoulders and back and then my bottom. He was especially thorough in applying a great deal of lotion to my bum cheeks, even getting it nice and evenly spread between the furrow, as if the sun's rays might penetrate into that darkest of places. I twitched when his massaging fingers came closer and closer to my anus, then pressed down on it, smothering it in cream, but I didn't protest. My body was his.

His lotioned hands slid in between my thighs, coating them completely.

'I wonder if anyone's ever had a sunburnt clit,' he said idly, sweeping his thumb swiftly but with devastating effect over mine.

Oh, I wanted him to touch it again, but he wouldn't.

'It seems a bit silly,' he said, grabbing me suddenly by the hips and positioning me over his lap, 'to put all that cream on your bottom to avoid sunburn when I'm going to get it bright red anyway.'

'Oh,' I mewled, on high alert. Even though I'd been expecting this, it still came as a shock somehow.

'I'm afraid the lotion might make it sting all the more,' he said. 'But perhaps you'll think of that next time you're running late.'

His hand smacked down and he was right – it did hurt quite a lot.

I let out an uninhibited yell. On the lake, some water birds wheezed and quacked and feathers flapped.

'You're getting off lightly,' he informed me, continuing the spanking at a brisk pace. My punishment was being observed by a gaggle of interested ducks and I imagined Will's eyes in the bushes, watching Jasper's hand fall over and over, hard and strong, on my rapidly heating arse.

'Ouch,' was about the only reply possible.

'I once took a girl down here,' he reminisced. 'An experienced submissive, she was. I wouldn't do this kind of thing with you yet. I took her down to the water's edge.'

The spreading sting of my hot, slippery bottom, together with the continuing hail of smacks, made it hard to focus on anything else, but I tried my best to follow Jasper's anecdote anyway.

'I gave her a pair of gloves to put on, then I made her pick a handful of nettles.'

'Oh, God. I hate them.' Childhood memories of being stung on the legs while I tried to negotiate an overgrown footpath crowded into my mind, adding somehow to the pain I was already experiencing.

'Yes, so did she.' He took some time to enjoy his memory, though the spanking carried on, its sound effects echoing over the lake until I thought it must be making ripples. 'I made her lie on the rug and I put the gloves on and I pressed them on to her arse cheeks. My God, did she wriggle and thrash. The sting lasted hours, she said. But it made her ragingly horny. She got quite into it, after that. Used to like it when I made her stuff them down her knickers and wear them to the shops. We'd always end up having to take a break for a quickie in the car.'

The spanking stopped abruptly, Jasper appearing to need a moment or two to recover from his tantalising tale.

I thought about his ex-lovers. Were there many? Did they satisfy him better than I could? The sting of this thought exceeded anything my bottom might endure, though my bottom was admittedly red hot by now and I was ready for a lull.

'Well,' he said, tapping at my sore cheeks. 'Maybe another time. Would you consider it?'

'I might,' I said, feeling that some stakes had been raised and staying in the game mattered more than anything.

'Brave girl,' he said. 'You're very, very red. It doesn't take much with you. I suppose because you're new to all this. Did you learn your lesson?'

'Yes, Sir.'

'That was a punishment, pure and simple. But I can make it a lot more pleasurable than that. I'll show you, maybe tonight.'

'Tonight?' I gritted my teeth at the thought of another spanking, so soon.

He stroked my tender skin.

'This won't last long,' he said, somewhat regretfully. 'You'll have forgotten it happened by tonight.'

I rather thought not, but didn't think contradicting him would be wise.

'Of course, the lotion makes it worse. Perhaps I should put some more on now. I seem to have spanked it all off.'

I lay over his lap while he rubbed still more lotion, blissfully cool and soothing, into my punished posterior.

'How's that?' he whispered.

I could tell how it was for him. A substantial bulge had been growing and hardening under my stomach throughout the spanking, and now it seemed to have reached critical mass.

'Very good, Sir,' I replied. 'So good. Oh, God.'

'As good as that?' His fingers skirted the edges of my sex, so near and yet so far. I whimpered and jiggled my hips. 'Do you know, I've known girls who could come just from being spanked. Isn't that amazing? Or the idea of it. Didn't even need to touch them.'

I was beginning to tire of his tales of super-duper submissives, to be honest. Why hold up these impossible paragons that I could never hope to emulate? It was irritating.

'Bully for them,' I snarked.

His massaging fingers stopped their work.

'Talk to me,' he said commandingly.

'I ... what? About what?'

'What's upsetting you? You'll find that honesty is the cornerstone of a D/s relationship, my love. I won't put up with passive-aggressive nonsense, or bottled up emotions. Everything has to be out in the open, or the whole dynamic gets hopelessly corrupted.'

'It's nothing.'

He smacked my bum so hard and so unexpectedly that I kicked the picnic basket over.

'Don't lie,' he hissed. 'Now come on. Out with it.'

'Just … you've had lots of experience and I've got none. And I feel like sometimes you might be goading me … a bit.'

'By telling you about other lovers I've had?'

'By telling me how bloody brilliantly submissive and sexy they were. Compared to me.'

'Oh, but I'm not comparing them to you at all. That's not what I'm doing. I'm just telling you what's possible, giving you a bit of insight into the BDSM world. I don't give a flying fuck whether you do any of those things or not.'

'Really?'

'Really. You have to find your own way. I'm here to help you with that. I'd like it if your way was my way, but it's much too early to tell on that front. We might be perfectly suited, we might not. You might want certain things I can't give you – who knows what's going to happen? This is a journey with no fixed destination.'

'You don't wish I was one of your superfreak exes?'

'Christ, no. You're you, and I like you. Essentially, you can take a good spanking and you're happy to be fucked morning, noon and night, so you'll do very well for me.'

'Mr Romantic.'

He laughed.

'I think it's romantic.'

'You're not normal.'

'No, but neither are you, my love. That's why we're here like this today, with you arse-up over my lap in the open air and me trying to work out how I can stop you spouting insecure angst for long enough to shag you senseless.'

My pussy tightened, longing for his touch. 'Oh, I hate you,' I moaned.

'But you want me,' he whispered, granting the lightest of touches to my clit. 'Don't you?'

I nodded, unable to escape the fact.

'I love that this is all new to you,' he said. 'But it's a little scary for me too.'

He pushed his fingers in further and I melted into a puddle of lust.

'Uh?' was all I could say.

'Being your first dominant lover. What if I put a foot wrong and taint the experience for you? I don't want to do that. So you have to tell me, you understand? You have to tell me the minute something feels wrong. You promise you'll do that?'

'I promise. Oh.'

His fingers slipped inside me, testing my readiness.

'I guess this isn't feeling wrong, though,' he said.

101

'Judging by how wet you are. Punishment turns you on, I see. I'll make it harder next time.'

He pulled out his fingers and displaced me from his lap.

'OK, kitten,' he said. 'On all fours now.'

A light breeze blew over me, making my nipples throb, as I positioned myself according to his requirements. I was facing the lake, and I pushed out my rear, imagining Will's eyes upon it, watching from the trees. He would know what was about to happen to me. He would see Jasper, getting the condom out of his jacket pocket, then unbuckling his belt, lowering his trousers, all the things he was doing that I could only hear and infer.

He would see Jasper's erect cock, see the condom going on, see my thighs spread wide and ready, see my scarlet bottom cheeks thrust out so Jasper could admire his handiwork while he rode me.

My lover's hands took my hips, then the rounded, wide head of his cock pushed at my cunt.

'I'm going to make you feel this,' he said. 'It's going deep.'

He screwed it into me, and he was right. He seemed to plumb depths previously unreached, stretching me to my limit.

Every thrust made me release a small moan, as if I was surprised, but I was not. It was simply that I had to do it, had to express some reaction to the intensity of the experience, had to make him know the effect he had on me.

The angle of penetration caused each forward sweep to glance upon my G-spot and the tight knot in my lower stomach soon began to unravel, gathering momentum with each hard impalement, each whispered obscenity, each grab of breast or bite of shoulder.

It was almost too late when I remembered I was supposed to ask permission for my orgasm.

'Are you feeling it?' Jasper's voice was hot and evil in my ear.

'God, yes, I'm going to ... may I ...?'

'Come.'

Oh, thank God. I fell forward, but he held me up, one hand on my shoulder, another around my waist, supporting me through the showers of stars and sparks. As it hit me, I remembered my manners and I howled, 'Thank you, Sir,' over and over again.

This pleased him; I could tell by the way he began slamming into me, whispering things I could barely make out, pinching his fingers down hard on my shoulder and then roaring over the lake, sending the waterfowl into another flapping panic.

We fell forward in a tangled crush of bodies. His weight pinned me to the rug and I felt his breath, rushes of heat on the back of my neck that grew longer and lighter over time.

'You must be starving,' he said eventually, rising slowly to his knees and reaching for the picnic basket. 'I know I am.'

He pulled out a bottle of champagne and got to work on the cork.

I wasn't sure I could move, so I stayed prone, resting my head on my hands, trying to work out if my bottom was still sore. I couldn't really tell. It seemed he was right about it fading fast.

'You look wrecked,' commented Jasper.

The cork popped.

'I am wrecked,' I said.

'After one go? That's no good. You need to get into training, my dear. Build up your stamina. Perhaps you should come running with me.'

Ugh. No thanks.

'I always hated PE at school,' I said. 'Nobody ever picked me because I was so weedy and badly co-ordinated. Terrible ball skills.'

'I wouldn't say that.' He grinned cheesily. 'I'm sure we can sort something out. Turn over, on to your back. Go on.'

I braved my protesting muscles and rolled myself over. Before I could sit up or register what was happening, Jasper had splashed champagne all over my breasts. I squealed and flapped my hands, but I was too late, for he had bent over me to lick it up. I had no idea how it would taste mixed with sun lotion – presumably not very nice, because he was grimacing when he raised his head again.

'Forgot about the lotion,' he said, wiping his mouth with his hand. 'I need something to take the taste away now.'

I laughed and laughed as he scrabbled through the picnic box looking for something to alleviate his flavour-related distress. He was habitually so cool and suave, it was really cheering to see him at a disadvantage for once.

'Are you laughing at me, Sarah?' He took a large bite of a pork pie.

I shook my head overdramatically.

'I would never laugh at you,' I lied.

He smacked at my thigh, just hard enough to get my attention and turn my laugh into a squeak.

'That's not true, is it? I thought we talked about honesty.'

'OK. I was laughing at you. It was funny, though.'

'I'll let you off this once.' He passed me the basket. 'Come on, get some meat in you.' He winked salaciously.

'You should direct a Carry On film,' I said, sitting up. 'And write the script. You seem to have all the innuendoes covered.'

'You know, I like that idea.' He took another bite of his pie and looked out to the lake, eyes narrowed. 'Bit of a departure from my normal style but I think it could work. Carry On Boffing.'

I snorted. '*Carry On Thrashing.*'

'*Carry On* meets *Fifty Shades of Grey.*'

'Oh God. Have you read it?'

'Read it? She wrote it about me, didn't she? I'm a mysterious billionaire. Well, I'm not a billionaire, to be honest, but that was just a bit of artistic licence. She meant me really.'

'You …' Perhaps I shouldn't call him a knob. Might be construed as disrespectful. I still struggled with his switches in tone, from dominant to playful in the blink of an eye.

'Don't you believe me?'

'You don't have a helipad on the roof,' I pointed out.

'Ah. Busted.'

'Do you have the dark, tormented past, though?'

'Yeah, I do, as it happens.' He paused and gave me a troubled look. My fingers tightened around my sausage roll. 'I once played a junior houseman in Broken Heart Surgery. Don't you remember?'

I burst out laughing and threw my sausage roll at him.

'Oh, why did you have to do that, my bad little kitten, oh, why?' He crawled towards me, his eyes gleaming, ready to pounce. I leaped to my feet and ran towards the lake, still laughing, squealing every now and then when I looked back to find him that little bit closer.

He lifted me clear of the ground and flung me over his shoulder. He was still naked from the waist down and he waded into the lake with me while I yelped and tried to catch my breath, boundlessly exhilarated.

'Don't throw me in,' I pleaded.

'Is that an order?' he asked, wheeling around so I nearly slid off his shoulder and had to clutch at his shirt collar. 'I don't take kindly to those.'

My only reply was a scream. I was sure I was about to fall.

'What's the matter? The water's lovely,' he teased.

'It's full of weeds,' I gasped.

'What are weeds going to do to you? Wrap themselves around you and tie you up? Actually … I like that image. Maybe I'll get a big handful of weeds and bind you tight with them. Bindweed.'

'They're slimy. No! Don't drop me!'

Too late. He bent forward and tipped me off him so I fell back into the shallow, muddy water with a splash and a spluttery yelp. At least I managed to soak his shirt, which gave me a small element of satisfaction.

'Right,' he said. 'I'll give you a head start. I'll count to twenty. You have to get as far away from me as you can.'

I answered as best I could with my nose full of water.

I said, 'Nnrught,' and I began wading towards the shore, cursing the water's weight against my thighs, wanting to take off into the air.

I heard his counting, calm and slow, and it made me rush so that I stumbled and lost time. I grabbed at the rushes, but they slid through my hands, and then one of them cut me. All I could do was rely on my feet, squelching through the sucking mud.

I was at the shore by the time he reached twenty, and then I realised I'd done it all wrong. I would never be able to beat him on land. The water was my only chance.

I began to skirt the edge of the lake, but he was on his way over, smiling in premature victory.

'Run, little rabbit, run,' he goaded, reaching out for me.

I tried, scooping up handfuls of water and splashing them towards him, but they all fell short of his advancing figure. He was going to get me. I might as well accept it.

And besides … I wanted him to.

But he mustn't know it. It wouldn't be so much fun if he knew it.

Soon enough, he was close enough to reach out for me. We twisted and flailed in a complicated waterlogged ballet, him lunging, me ducking, until an overhead bramble caught his hair and held him back for valuable seconds.

Making good my advantage, I scrambled through the reeds and up to the shore, where I hid on the far side of the thicket that had slowed him down. A weeping willow hung over the bank and I snapped off a wand of it, thinking that a weapon might come in handy.

Rustling and snapping of twigs heralded his return to the fray. I tried to conceal myself deep in the undergrowth, but he must have seen me, because his creeping footsteps were most definitely heading in my direction.

I leaped to my feet and brandished my willow wand, swooshing it about in the air. The noise triggered a spark of arousal, and I realised it would make rather a fiendish whip. And if I'd realised that, then Jasper …

He laughed.

'Bad mistake, Sarah,' he said. 'Very, very bad.'

I cracked it towards him. He wouldn't dare come too near, especially with his lower half completely naked.

He held up his hands.

'I don't think you want to do that,' he cautioned. 'Put it down.'

I waved it desperately.

He stepped closer, holding out his hand.

'Give it to me.'

I shook my head and leaped back.

'Give it to me now and I'll go easy on you.'

I simply lashed the air with it and took to my heels, up the grassy slopes, away from the trees, towards the picnic rug.

My breath was painful in my chest and my thighs were starting to give up the ghost when he caught me, less than halfway up the hill, grabbing at my upper arm. I tried to flick the willow back at him, but he got hold of that too and wrested it away from me with insulting ease.

'Oh dear,' he gloated into my ear, wrapping his arm around my stomach and clamping me against him. 'I thought you'd make more of an effort. You definitely need to come running with me.'

'It's not fair,' I moaned, making feeble token attempts to extricate myself. 'I stood no chance.'

'I know.' He kissed the hollow beneath my earlobe. 'Poor Sarah. Now you're my prisoner. What shall I do with you?'

'I suppose you'll do whatever you want.'

'I suppose I will. Come on then.'

He marched me back to the picnic blanket and made me get on all fours, head down between my elbows, back sloping up from my neck so that my bottom was pushed right out.

'This is quite a weapon.' He swished the willow wand through the air. The sound, so invigorating when it came from my own hand, was now terrifying. 'A slash across the face could have been very nasty. And I'm sure you've no idea how to wield it. Have you?'

'Not really,' I admitted. 'Are you going to …?'

'I think I'm going to have to, aren't I? Or how are you ever going to learn your lesson?'

'Oh.'

I think he must have picked up the fear in my voice, because he brushed the switch over my bottom, quite gently.

'Don't be afraid,' he said. 'I'm an expert. I won't go too far.'

How far was too far?

He performed the merest flick of the wrist and the end of the wand snapped sweetly on to my rear. It was a sizzling caress, nothing more, and it made me sigh.

'More of that, eh?' he said.

'Mmm.'

But more of that wasn't on the agenda. Instead he drew his arm much further back and whipped me properly, drawing a glowing line on my bum.

I jolted forward and screeched. It really, really hurt.

'Not what you expected?' he asked smoothly.

'It burns.'

'A nice, lasting burn. How many do you think you can take?'

'I'm not sure.' Now the immediate shock was past, I found myself enjoying the residual throb. 'Maybe you could try another.'

He snorted. 'Maybe I could.'

He did. It sliced across the top of the previous stripe, convincing me that I had made the wrong decision.

And yet, I kept on making that wrong decision. I kept bringing the safeword to the tip of my tongue, then swallowing it.

No matter how many times I sucked in my breath and gripped at the rug and wobbled on my knees, I went back for more, pushing my bum back out, doing what he wanted me to do.

Somehow I suffered through ten strokes of fiendish, furious pain before begging for mercy.

He threw the switch aside, pulled me up to a kneeling position and kissed me so fervently that I forgot all about the pulsing and the heat behind. Or at least, I did until its effects bled into my clit and my pussy, combining with the kiss to set me aflame. He cupped my arse cheeks, squeezing and running his thumbs over the welts, while his tongue plunged further.

'Want you,' he gasped, breaking free. 'Here.'

He lay back, dealt with the rubber and moved me over his upright cock, lowering me down with teasing slowness until I had him exactly where I wanted him, right up inside me. I began to grind slowly, bending low to brush my nipples against his wet shirt, and he let me for a little while before pinching my hips to make me stop.

'Turn around,' he whispered. 'I want to see your marks while I'm fucking you.'

Oh God. I was so stuffed full of delirious, submissive lust that I would have done anything he asked, but this was a gymnastic move beyond my capability. Or so I thought.

I worked, slowly and carefully, at rotating myself one

hundred and eighty degrees, his cock the screw, my cunt the nut. Never was a tool more delicately secured.

Finally, after much balancing of limbs, I found myself facing his feet. His cock felt strange at this angle – upside-down. I felt I ought to lean back or I might warp it out of shape.

But he seemed happy enough. Instead, at his behest, I bent forward and he kept his hold of my hips.

'That's it,' he said. 'I can see them all now. Ten red stripes. That must hurt.'

He pressed his finger into one and I winced.

'It's … really … sore,' I gasped, feeling his cock, thick and fat, stretching my boundaries.

'Good,' he said, long and low, almost orgasmically. 'You don't know how much that turns me on. Come on. Work that cunt, Sarah.'

My thighs were starting to ache but I kept a rhythmic pressure on his shaft, back and forth, bearing down where it crossed my G-spot.

He prodded and pinched at my arse while he screwed me, as if trying to push me through my barriers, on to a higher level of physical fitness. The idea that he was some kind of kinky personal trainer flashed into my mind, and I imagined myself on a treadmill, panting and sweating just as I was now, while he whipped me into shape.

The need to ask permission for my orgasm was becoming urgent. I braced my palms flat between his legs, holding myself up while I edged towards the point of no return.

'You're getting it now,' he said. 'Getting what you asked for.'

'Please, Sir,' I squeaked.

'No,' he said, thrusting harder.

'Oh, pleeeease.' I smacked at the ground, not sure it was possible to obey him.

'You don't deserve it,' he panted. 'Running away from me like that.'

'Oh, but it was a game. Please! Let me come.'

'It's all a game, Sarah. And I make the rules.'

I nearly screamed with frustration and laid my head on the ground. Behind me, he gathered pace and stormed into his climax, digging his fingers hard into my upper thighs and bottom.

I wriggled futilely on his still hard cock. He laughed and slapped my bum.

'Poor Sarah,' he said. Then, 'Off you pop.'

My cunt raging, I disengaged and wiped my eyes and brow. The sweat was running into my switch marks, making the burn double in intensity. My clit felt so big I could barely press my thighs together. I was a melting, stinging, pulsing mess.

Jasper lay, recovering, for a little while, eyes shut, infuriatingly relaxed and at peace. I wanted to kick him.

His eyes opened again.

'Pack the basket,' he said. 'Picnic's over.'

I tried not to look too overtly rebellious, but I might have flung the items into the hamper a little more roughly than necessary.

Jasper put his trousers back on, though my clothes were packed up with the plates and glasses, and picked up the switch.

'Let's go,' he said, flicking it at my upper thighs so I jumped forward, startled.

We walked back to the house like this, me naked and in front, while he chivvied me on with little cuts to my legs and bottom, holding the picnic basket in his other arm. When we passed through the wooded area where I'd encountered Will, I wanted to cover myself, and looked furtively to either side for signs of an observer. I saw nobody, but every little noise made my heart flip.

Back at the house, Jasper took pity on me. He made me bend over the arm of a chair while he used a dildo, sliding it in and out and over my slippery clit with tight control until I came, hard, saying his name.

He made me spend the rest of the afternoon in the corner of his study with my hands on my head while he dealt with correspondence and phone calls.

I could see through the window if I moved my eyes to the right and, at one point, I thought I detected movements, out by the old stables.

But I could have been dreaming.

Chapter Five

The summer came and it stayed, graciously for an English season.

I would spend the hottest part of the day indoors with my cataloguing, but in the mornings I was often found in the overgrown gardens, wearing a tiny flirty near-transparent dress Jasper had bought online. The overblown roses brushed my thighs as I passed them and sometimes their thorns would prick. I would shut my eyes and breathe in, honeysuckle, jasmine, and a ripe lusciousness behind all the scents. Life, languor, summer, sex.

I stopped putting my hair up and let it fall anyhow, spilling over my shoulders and flicking my breasts. My limbs went from alabaster to tan, and I seemed to follow in their wake, from academic to wood nymph.

Jasper rarely accompanied me on these garden trips, and, besides, we were usually in recovery from some bout of epic kinky sex. As I wandered about the holly-hocks and foxgloves, he would be pounding around the perimeter of the estate, intent on maintaining his stamina. He had a lot of it.

The birds would sing and the petals would fall and I would sit on the garden bench and dream. What did I dream about? I dreamed that this would never end.

Once the artefacts were put back in their cabinets for the afternoon, it was time for the game. The game of master and servant, dominant and submissive. The best game in the world, infinite in its variety.

Every day brought something different, a new twist or take. Jasper, as befitted a man who made stories real for a living, possessed a jewel of an imagination.

One evening, I was a harem slave and he my prince, choosing me for the night, oiling me up, making me perform lewd acts for him while he lazed on a cushion, directing the action.

Another day I found myself suspended by my wrists in chains from the cellar ceiling while he introduced me to the dubious pleasures of the clover clamp.

I was a blindfolded prisoner brought up for punish-ment; a careless maid who needed to be made an example of; a proud lady blackmailed into humility by a wicked baronet. I was all of these and more. I'd never been one

117

for drama, but Jasper drew these performances from me with ease. He was the consummate director.

Afterwards he would bathe me, rub soothing ointment into my bottom (or wherever it was needed), hold me in his arms, let me sail into sleep with him.

Nobody and nothing broke into our fantasy world.

When he took calls, he never told me what they were about. Now and again he went to London for the day, but I didn't question him about his business. We were in a bubble: a perfect, shiny, fragile but all-encompassing bubble. I could think of no better place to be.

A humid July burnt off into a scratchy, thirsty August.

The petals dried and the skies hurt my eyes. Everything was bleached and desiccated; the waters of the lake were low.

On a day like this, I was ordered upstairs after lunch to change. He had bought me something, I surmised, and I was right. Laid out on my bed I found a set of riding gear. Jodhpurs, long-sleeved white top, hard hat, mouth-watering shiny boots.

It looked like a ride was in prospect.

This was odd, though, because, while the estate had stables, there were no horses. I had never ridden, being nervous of their size and their teeth.

Nonetheless, I pulled on the jodhpurs, smiling in advance at how Jasper was going to like the way they clung to every curve and accentuated the shape of my arse. The top went on next, and now I really hoped the ride, if it happened, might be a slow and stately trot because the thought of my bra-less breasts bouncing about on horseback made me cringe.

The boots fit precisely. The leather shone like twin mirrors. I watched myself put on the hard hat, looking down at my feet, then I saluted myself, took a final twirl and headed for Jasper.

He stood in the hallway, smart as the whip he held, in a dark riding jacket with brass buttons. I thought it must surely be too hot for the breathless weather, but he didn't seem concerned. His boots were even shinier than mine and he looked slick, ruthless and jodhpur-dampeningly sexy.

'Are you ready to ride?' he asked me, slapping the crop down in the palm of one hand.

'I'm ... not sure, Sir.' We'd come to an arrangement whereby he was 'Sir' after four o'clock, 'Jasper' before.

'Have you ridden before?'

'No, never.'

'What, not even a pony?'

'Not even a seaside donkey.'

'Well, we'll have to fix that. Come on.'

He patted my bottom with the whip, gently but firmly, ushering me through the front door.

'I didn't think you had a horse,' I said, as he steered me around the side of the house towards the stables.

119

'I don't. This is on loan for the day, from a friend.'

'Oh. Wow.' On approaching the stables it became clear that a real horse was indeed in situ. I heard it snort, then saw it shake its head through the top of the half-door. 'But there's only one.'

'Well spotted. Yes, there's only one.'

We stopped at the stable door. Jasper patted the horse's nose and gave him half an apple he'd had in his pocket.

'So … are we both going on the same horse? Or …?'

'What's going to happen, Sarah, is that you are my stable girl, and you're going to saddle and bridle my horse. Of course, since you're very inexperienced, I've no doubt you'll make a horrible mess of it. Oh dear.'

He waved at some harness-type stuff, hanging on pegs.

'Give it your best shot,' he said, retiring to sit cross-legged on a hay bale.

'What if it kicks me?' I asked dubiously.

'Stay near his head. You'll be fine.'

I had all kinds of reservations about this, but I took the tack from the pegs, buckling slightly under its unexpected weight, and carried it into the stall.

'Hi, horse,' I said warily. 'We're going to be friends, aren't we?' I put my hand on his face, trying not to transmit waves of fear to him.

Where to start? I picked up the saddle and sort of hoisted it over the horse's back. He was surprisingly docile about it all and made no attempt to rear up and kick me in the eye. But I was supposed to fasten it underneath. It all seemed much too risky and complicated. I tried to reach for the straps, but with each attempt I found myself shying away at the last minute.

Jasper, on his hay bale, laughed and tapped the crop against his calf.

I thought perhaps I'd leave that until later, and picked up the bridle instead. Oh, God. This thing was way, way too complicated. How did it fit? How did one put it on? I spent a ridiculous amount of time trying to slide it over the horse's ears, but he wasn't keen and kept tossing his head. After the fifth attempt, Jasper lost patience and came to join me.

'They said you knew how to tack up a horse,' he said, finishing off the job himself while I slumped against the stable door. 'What's this supposed to be?'

'Sorry, Sir.'

'I should think so. Your reference was good. Did you forge it?'

'No!'

'I'm going to call Mrs Horse-Whisperer and ask her over the phone.'

'Oh, no, don't do that,' I said, cottoning on to the scene.

'Why not?' He paused in the straightening of the harness and gave me a hard stare.

'Because ... because ... she's on holiday.'

'No, she isn't.'

121

'I'm sorry, Sir,' I mumbled.

'So you did forge it?'

I nodded, kicking my heel against the stable door.

He finished with the bridle before saying, 'I see. Why?'

'Needed a job, Sir.'

'A job you aren't qualified to do.'

'I can learn.'

'Yes.' He looked up from fiddling with the saddle strap. 'Yes, you can learn. And you will learn. You'll learn what happens to little liars.'

'Oh, please don't sack me!'

'I'm not going to sack you. Like you said, you can learn. Do you want to learn?'

'Y-yes, Sir.' I pretended to have no idea what was coming but of course I did.

'Good. So you can go and bend over those hay bales there.'

'Bend over them?'

'That's right. I want you bent over with your bottom pushed right out in those nice tight jodhpurs.'

'What are you ... going to do?'

'What does it sound like?' He tapped the crop, with a light thwack, against his thigh.

I quailed.

'Are you going to use ... that?'

'Too many questions. There's only one way to find out. Go and bend over.'

What would be going through a girl's head in this situation? Fear, bemusement, disbelief. I tried to replicate it all as I headed for the bales, highly conscious of how the jodhpurs clung to my backside.

He'd stacked these bales to exactly the right height and put a horse blanket over the top so as not to prickle my skin, if the time came for it to be bared.

I tipped myself forward, feeling the material stretch tight across my spreading cheeks. It wasn't going to offer much protection, especially with no knickers underneath. He'd be able to see the outline of my pussy.

'What do you have to say to me?' he asked, looming behind me.

'I'm very sorry, Sir,' I said. 'Please … do you have to?'

'It's for your own good, young lady,' he said, words which always unleashed the flood down below. 'If I let you off, I won't be doing you any favours. You need to understand the importance of honesty.'

There was nothing to be said. Instead of framing useless words, I let my mouth concentrate on pinching my lips together while the rest of my body went into preparation mode.

I had learned, over these weeks, not to tense up too much. It had been a hard road, but Jasper didn't tolerate the clenching of buttocks during a spanking, and I had finally found the knack of keeping myself loose and breathing through it all.

It would be all right, I told myself. It would hurt, but it wouldn't last long, and then I would have the glorious after-effects to enjoy. But the glorious after-effects only came with a fairly severe thrashing, so I had to pace myself and take as much as I could.

I was expecting the whip, but he started with his hand. The sound his palm made on my taut clothed bottom was like a series of pistol shots. The horse whinnied, perhaps wondering what the hell was going on. Or maybe he'd seen it all before.

Jasper kept the pressure up, spanking hard and resolutely, covering every inch of my bottom and then down to mid-thigh. I was already hot and my clothes were tight and it didn't take long for me to feel uncomfortably roasted. I fretted that my jodhpurs would have to be peeled down, stuck to my bum by the adhesive heat of the spanking and my own juices. Besides that, my cunt was prickling, my clit swollen, pushing against the fabric. I pictured it, a fat round shape visible through the stretch-cotton.

Perhaps if I wiggled my hips just a bit, I could get a bit of friction going …

But I didn't dare. Jasper would know, and he'd punish me.

He stayed his hand at last and I was able to try and steady myself.

'My hand's sore,' he remarked. 'Which isn't really the idea. I think it's time for something a little stronger.'

124

This would be the crop, for sure.

Unsurprisingly, it was an antique number, one of several in his possession. This particular one was closer to a whip than the others, having a silver cap with a wrist strap attached, a grip of braided leather, a shaft of slender, flexible cane and a heavy leather loop at the end.

Jasper had educated me on the uses of horsewhips. Apparently, the loop was to keep hounds from jumping up at the horses during a hunt. It also made the most diabolical cracking sound when he swished it through the air. And it was very painful to be struck with, although not quite as painful as the shaft of the whip, which I had also experienced.

I felt the loop drift down the cleft of my bottom, which the jodhpurs made rudely apparent, and rub lazily against my hot pussy. I gasped and rotated my hips. Gently as he did it, it would not take much of that to send me over the edge.

He tutted and retracted it.

'You'll stain those jodhpurs,' he reproved.

Then there was a whoosh and I almost clenched, but remembered myself just in time to feel the blazing splat full on the centre of my backside, a heavy kind of sting that penetrated my flesh.

'Twenty of these to start,' he said. 'Keep that arse high.'

I pushed it back out and waited for more. I got it. The leather loop fell full-force another nineteen times, burning my tight trousers on to my skin. I was made to push myself out and spread my cheeks wide until I was sure the fabric would split, but it never did, just stretched and stretched while the whip was plied over and over.

After the twenty strokes were laid, he pulled down the jodhpurs, easing them slowly over my sore bottom, right down to the tops of my boots.

'Good and red all over,' he applauded himself, feeling the heat with both palms. 'But I haven't finished with you yet. Twenty more on your bare bottom. Nice and high, please.'

I felt these more acutely, each hard stroke searing and welting my skin so I knew my arse would be dark red and swollen before too long. That antique leather, although supple, had a particular weight that made it one of the worst weapons in Jasper's armoury. I was yelling out and pleading (though not safewording) by the sixth stroke.

By twenty, I had tears in my eyes and my pussy was awash in my juices. The fire consumed me, its flames licking every part of my body.

'Are you learning your lesson?' asked Jasper. 'That looks very sore.' He sucked in a breath and tutted, running his fingers around the ridges and bumps he had wrought.

'Yes, Sir,' I moaned.

'Good,' he said. His fingers prodded between my lower lips. 'Christ, you're wet, girl. Very wet.'

I pushed myself back on them, desperate for stimulation.

'I don't know if I should,' he whispered. 'But …'

I heard him pull down his own jodhpurs, and then his cock head swirled around in my wetness. (We had had tests done, at his insistence, in a local private clinic and there was no further need for condoms.)

'Oh, please,' I begged, my voice quivering.

He entered, an inch, then stopped.

'Oh, more, please.'

He did this several times, moving further in then waiting for me to beg, until he was all the way in.

I sighed with relief, more than ready for my punishment fuck.

But he thrust no more than three times before pulling out again and saying, 'No, not yet. You need more whipping first.'

'Oh, but, Sir,' I almost screamed.

'Ten more. And I'm taking off the loop.'

My boiling blood froze. This would really, really hurt. Without the loop, the crop was as bad as the cane, if not more so.

'Oh, no,' I whimpered.

'You'll count these,' he said. 'And every stroke will

teach you to be truthful with me. Because if I catch you in any more lies, this will seem like a gentle caress.'

I summoned up all my spirit, all my will, all my courage. I would live through this. I could always safeword but, if I did, I wouldn't have quite the quality of afterburn and exquisite soreness I wanted. I would think of that, and of the frantic sex afterwards, Jasper's pelvis slapping against my welts, the sweat adding more sweet sting.

I concentrated hard on these thoughts, and each eye-watering stroke of the whip handle was bearable, even welcome. I let the shock shudder through me, let the fire burn pure and bright, then lessen by degrees, until ten bright red lines were written on my backside. Jasper's signature, marks of ownership I bore with pride and love.

'Ten, Sir,' I whispered, my voice shaky and cracked but still there somehow.

'Truth, Sarah,' he said, bending over me to speak low in my ear. 'How do you feel?'

I felt disconnected from the earth, floating happily inside my pain and submission.

'Amazing,' I sighed.

He kissed my neck.

'Spread your legs as wide as you can, love.'

I was grateful of the hay bale to lean on or I would have fallen over. My legs were in no fit state to support my weight now. Jasper grabbed hold of my hips and slid in to the hilt without ceremony, holding me fast against the haystack so that my legs were prickled by straw. He began a hard, fast slamming, slapping into my burning bum, bringing his own extra heat and sting to proceedings.

'Oh yes,' he said through gritted teeth. 'This wasn't in the reference either but you can do it, can't you? I'll put that in your next one. Sarah might not be able to saddle a horse but she can take a good hard fucking. She can spread her legs and take it, even when her arse has been whipped.'

I shut my eyes and flew into space. The full force of my orgasm hit me a minute or so later, but I was too weak to do anything but let it take me, lying like a rag doll while Jasper pounded into me then filled my cunt with his spunk.

The front of his body moulded to the curve of my spine while he lay, spent, his face beside mine on the blanket.

'Sarah,' he whispered.

He had clasped his hands together in front of my face and I laid my chin on them and turned to meet him in a kiss.

We were both too tired to speak, but the kiss took what breath we had and turned it into something more eloquent than words. I sent him my love and he sent it back, by way of skin on skin and tongue against tongue.

'Stay with me,' he said softly, breaking apart.

I didn't want to ask what he meant by that, in case it wasn't what I wanted him to mean. I just shut my eyes and nodded and laid my cheek on the blanket again.

'You make me cruel,' he said. 'You make me want to do the worst things to you.'

'I know.'

He pulled out of me and sorted out his clothes then, somewhat to my horror, he reached down to pull up my jodhpurs.

Oh, they were far too tight and uncomfortable to wear now!

But he ignored my squirming legs and pulled them up my damp thighs, over the two cane strokes that lay upon them, and then set the subsiding heat in my bum right back up to the top of the dial by yanking them up high and tight over the welts.

'Ow, oh, that's too hot,' I complained, shimmying my hips wildly.

'I want you to feel it,' he said, patting my bottom.

Between my legs, his semen trickled out of me, staining the material and demanding my attention. I was squishy and hot and damp and sore and incredibly turned on again. He pulled me up straight and fondled my breasts, my stiff little nipples telling him what he needed to know.

'I can be as cruel as I like to you, can't I?' he said, biting my earlobe. 'You love it. Now I'm going to be even crueller.'

He pinched my nipples, walked back to the horse and tacked it up properly this time.

'Over here,' he said, extending a hand.

'I can't ride it,' I exclaimed. 'Not now!'

The thought of sitting on that unforgiving leather, bobbing up and down in the saddle on my tender, smarting, bruised bottom was quite horrible. And yet fascinatingly irresistible.

'You'll do as you're told, Sarah,' he said, reaching for the whip again.

I trotted over, post-haste, and let him hand me up on to the ludicrously tall beast until I sat uncertainly on top of it.

'Lean forward,' he said, and I did, feeling my pussy lips and clit crush up against the saddle, soaked in spunk. Meanwhile, my arse was on fire, throbbing like fury. I wanted to come again.

'I'll take the rein,' he said. 'I'm just going to take you on a nice long walk around the estate. All you need to do is hold on.'

I endured the maddening arousal all the way around the edges of the grounds, trying as hard as I could not to rub myself against the saddle, but my seat made it inevitable that certain kinds of friction were experienced and somewhere near the lake I lost control and clutched at the reins, whimpering.

Jasper, who had been recounting a long story about

131

learning to ride for a swashbuckling movie he filmed in the forests of Slovakia, stopped in mid-sentence and watched me, smiling widely.

'Poor thing,' he said. 'You've really lost control of yourself, haven't you? I think we'll need a few more training sessions this week.'

'I'm sorry, Sir,' I wailed, not wanting to go back to lying on my back with my legs spread in the air while Jasper used all kinds of vibrating and stimulating toys on me, withholding permission to come until the very last.

'I'm sure you are,' he said. 'OK, shuffle right forward. I'm going to get on behind you.'

I leaned right down, hanging on to the reins for dear life, while Jasper mounted at my rear. He pulled the reins tighter, dug in his heels and the horse set off at a pace I hadn't expected.

'Oh, God!' I jolted up and down, feeling every movement right down inside me.

Jasper had the horse canter all the way back to the stables, making me bump up and down and squeal with breathless fear.

I had never been more thankful to end a journey in my life. I was saddle-sore now, as well as whip-sore, and my jodhpurs felt like a horrible kind of heated second skin. My clit was raw and swollen from all the friction, and sweat trickled down the back of my neck.

Jasper took me back to the house and bathed me, then I was allowed to lie on my stomach on his bed while he fed me cold cuts and salad and fruit before rubbing heavenly cool lotion on to my still pulsing welts.

'I enjoyed that,' he said, a little unnecessarily, coming to lie beside me. 'Perhaps we should go riding more often.'

'I'm not sure I could cope with that every day,' I cautioned him.

'No, not every day,' he agreed. 'But next time I'd use a butt plug on you. I bet that'd be an interesting experience on horseback.'

I winced at the thought. We hadn't done butt plugs yet, but I was pretty sure that the day was close.

'Yes,' he said, after a moment's thought. 'I think butt plugs come next. Tomorrow. How do you feel about that?'

'How am I supposed to feel?'

'Apprehensive? Excited? Turned on?'

'That's how I feel all the time now.'

'Same here, Sarah. Same here.'

Chapter Six

The sun went in, the week after that, but the ground was still warm and the air still just this side of overripe on the day we made the film.

He promised me nobody would ever see it but, as we crossed towards the wood, him with camera and tripod, me carrying the box of props, I still had a few reservations.

'Are you sure nobody ever comes down here? Dog walkers? Poachers? Lost hikers?' Again I thought about telling him about Will, and again I chickened out.

'I've never seen or heard a soul,' he said. 'A few birds might witness your shame, but that's about it.'

'What are you going to do to me?'

'I'm not telling you. I want your reactions to be natural.'

134

We arrived in the glade and he started setting up. I put down my box and wandered around, peering between each tree, checking for telltale signs of hidden voyeurs.

I was still thus engaged when he called me back over.

'Right,' he said, holding the camera up to his eye. 'I want you to strip. You aren't wearing much so it won't take long.'

I grimaced and looked off to the side again, then pulled my T-shirt over my head, revealing my perennially bra-less breasts.

'Play with them,' he said. 'Touch your nipples.'

I cupped them in my hands and stroked my nipples with my thumbs. I couldn't look at the camera for this, until he commanded me to do so in a voice that brooked no refusal. So I gave him my sulkiest under-eyelid glare and carried on.

'Would you ever get your nipples pierced?' he asked.

I winced.

'I can't imagine it.'

'It would make them even more sensitive. And you could have little rings and I could put a chain through them and pull you along by it.'

I sucked air through my teeth. It all sounded very worrying. But if he wanted me to do it, I probably would.

'Or you could have little studs with my initials,' he said idly. 'Because they're mine, aren't they?'

'Yes, Sir.'

'Right, off with your skirt.'

It was a tiny mini anyway, barely covering anything. I slipped it down over my newly shaved pussy. I hoped he wasn't going to ask me about piercing *that*.

I stood back up in only stockings, suspenders and high heels and twisted my body round to the left, trying to get my face right out of shot.

'Are you hiding from me?' he asked in a teasing sing-song. 'Hide and seek. OK. Turn around then.'

I presented my back to him with some relief.

'I can see some little bruises on your bottom, Sarah. Some fading marks. I'm zooming in on them … nice and close up. Can you tell me when you got those?'

'You know when.'

'For the camera.'

'Three days ago.'

'And how did you get them?'

'I, uh, you did it.'

'I'm aware of that. How did I do it?'

'With a cane, Sir.'

'That's right. You got a good caning, didn't you? How many strokes?'

'Six, Sir.'

'Would you say they were six of the best?'

Unconsciously, I let my hands stray around to touch my bottom, reliving the hellish smart.

'No, I would say they were six of the worst.'

136

He laughed.

'Oh, that was nothing,' he promised. 'Nothing at all. Do they still hurt a little?'

'A little. I can sit down again.'

'For now.'

I sighed. 'Yes, Sir. For now.'

'It's a shame for your bottom that you can't keep out of trouble, isn't it, Sarah?'

'Yes, Sir.'

'Turn back round. No, don't put your hands there. Keep them at your sides. Spread your legs, wider. What have we here? Touch it.'

I put a fingertip on my clit, looking straight downwards.

'Let's play a guessing game,' he suggested. 'You've been here, what, six weeks?'

'Seven.'

'Seven weeks. Forty-nine days or so. How many times has that pussy been fucked in those seven weeks? What's your guess?'

'Oh, I don't know. Maybe ...' I tried a quick mental calculation. It was going to be a lot. Twice a day was slow. Sometimes he made it four or five.

'A hundred and fifty,' I guessed, as a safe average.

'Wow. You think that pussy has been fucked a hundred and fifty times since you got here. That's a hard-working pussy, isn't it? A greedy, rapacious but very hard-working little pussy. And I bet it isn't even tired, is it? I bet it wants more.'

'Maybe, Sir.'

He chuckled. 'Maybe? No two ways about it. I can see it glistening from here. How can we take your mind off it? Do some exercises. Star jumps. Go on. Give me twenty.'

Star jumps were not comfortable with no bra and my tits soon began to ache.

'OK, good. Now I want you to touch your toes, left to right, right to left, twenty times. Actually, turn around to do this. I want to watch your arse.'

I plunged down, ten times either side, watching the breeze in the trees, trying to pretend there was no camera.

'Now get down on the grass and give me ten sit-ups. With your hands behind your head. Spread your legs a bit, let me see if you're still wet. Oh dear, Sarah. What will it take? You're insatiable, aren't you? Get up then.'

I stood up, breathless and warmed up, my body tingling.

'I know you like things old school, love, and so do I. So I'm going to give you a penknife and ask you to cut yourself a nice switch. A good whippy one. Make sure it's got some staying power. If it breaks, you'll have to cut another and start all over again.'

He pulled a Swiss Army knife from his pocket – vintage, of course – and threw it at my feet. He followed me around the copse, camera in hand, while I tried to select a good switch. I knew it had to be flexible, not too brittle, which was difficult at this time of year. Most of the sap had dried out and the branches were snappy instead of swingy. But eventually I found a good birch rod, in one of the shadiest parts of the grove, and I sawed it off and cut away any knobbly bits or buds, just as Jasper had taught me.

All the while, his camera hovered at my shoulder and he asked me sly little questions. 'Why are you doing that? How will it affect the sensation? What's worse – a switch or a cane?'

I couldn't answer the last one. The cane laid ice that turned to fire and made ridges across my flesh, but the switch could make my bottom feel as if something hot and sharp had been embedded inside it for days on end.

'Now then,' he said. 'Carry on preparing that rod while I put the camera on the tripod. I'm in the next few scenes.'

I chipped away at my instrument of punishment until the camera angle was right and he had rolled up his shirtsleeves, ready. I loved that shirtsleeve moment; it never failed to make my heart flutter and my pussy clench.

'Hand me the switch,' he said grimly.

When I did so, he swished it through the air, nodded approvingly, then laid it aside, turning instead to the prop box. He took a length of rope, walked to a spreading chestnut tree and threw the rope over a low-hanging branch, securing it there with a complicated fastening. Then he beckoned me over.

He looped and knotted rope around both my wrists, shortening its length until my arms were raised and my hands rested just under the branch.

I stood, in my stockings, suspenders and heels, back to the camera, tethered to the tree. I could move about a foot in any direction, but no further.

'OK, now I've got you safe and secure,' he said, moving back to the prop box. I looked over my shoulder and saw that he held a squeezy tube of lubricant in one hand. I knew what was going to happen next, then.

I screwed up my face and waited.

He came close behind me and kissed the back of my neck, so softly, so gently, while his hand stroked my bottom, one finger travelling up and down the cleft, a little deeper each time, opening it with practised assurance.

'Do you know what's coming?' he whispered.

He stood a little to my side – that would be for the camera's benefit, so it could pick up a good clear shot of my spread cheeks.

'A plug?' I hazarded, hardly audibly.

'Clever girl.'

I heard him uncap the lubricant, then his

finger disappeared and, when it came back, it was cold and slippery and probed much more deeply and firmly. I remembered what to do, kept my muscles loose, let his fingertip enter the ring, up to the knuckle, and prepare me.

He narrated for the camera once it was inside, loudly and confidently.

'Sarah's relatively new to anal play,' he said, 'but she's learned to give her back passage up to me whenever I require it of her. I've trained her on different sized plugs and she can take quite a big one now. Like this one.'

Another pause for lubrication, then his finger popped out and a new, bigger, broader invader took its place. Now I really needed to keep calm, but I clenched my fists and curled my toes as my ring widened, and widened until the quick, fierce pain came. For a second it seemed unbearable, as it always did, and then the widest part was inside me and the flare receded and I felt only full and small and very humiliated.

Jasper held me by the hip as he fed the plug into my bum, making sure I didn't writhe or twist out of the way.

'This is a good one,' he said, kissing my neck again, ending with a sucking bite. 'You're going to feel this. Can you feel it?'

'I'm very full,' I whispered.

'Stuffed full,' he said with satisfaction. 'It's all the way in now.' He patted the flange and stood well aside. 'See, now she's ready.'

I heard his footprints on the dry grass, further away then closer again. He had the switch, I supposed.

'It's a shame I can only get this from one angle,' he remarked. 'Ideally, I need two cameras. One for your arse and one for your face. Or I should get a third party to film it. What do you think?'

'No!'

He laughed.

'It would be much better. Never mind. Now keep still as you can. This is going to hurt.'

The air whistled and then I cried out. The switch was intense, a slim slice of pure agony across the fleshiest part of my bottom. I almost felt the redness of it; it could properly be called a cut, even though the skin wasn't broken.

He lit my arse up with more, more, more. I swung and moaned, lifted my feet, rocked on my toes, yanked at my bonds, but I could not get away from the relentless swish, swish, swish and the subsequent sequence of throbs.

'You'll feel this for a while,' he said.

I began to notice, after five or so, how each stroke made the butt plug quiver inside me, sending a message to my cunt. Jasper began laying the thickest part of the switch heavily across the flange, which didn't sting so much but made shock waves radiate through the base of my belly and outwards.

142

'A paddle would be better for this,' he said, moving further back again and reverting to circus ringmaster mode. He had told me before about the importance of technique. A lesser dom might judge the stroke wrong and send the switch tip wrapping around my hip, which would be painful in a much less pleasurable way.

But Jasper was no lesser dom.

There was nothing in my life except the pain and the anticipation of the pain. Every other sense fell back into obscurity, in subjection to the whip and its ownership of me. This sharp, sweet smart at my rear was all I was. I let it govern me, ride my body and soul into another place, a place where Sarah was nothing, and ego didn't exist.

He showed me what I was – his.

I only realised after he stopped that my arms were aching and sweat was running down my thighs, mingled with my own sticky juices. The sensations of plugging and throbbing seemed to feed off each other, creating an arousal so almighty I rather feared the orgasm it would bring.

'Brave little Sarah.' His breath was hot in my ear.

He laid his hands on my welted arse and squeezed it so that a million pinpricks of extra pain rushed through me, catching up with the endorphins in a wild dance.

He put his mouth on the back of my neck and sucked, lusciously at first, then with deeper dedication. He was going to mark me, and I wanted him to. He could sink his teeth right into that tender flesh and I wouldn't flinch. He didn't, though – simply kept up the pressure on the side of my neck while one of his hands moved between my thighs and sought out my clit. It was easily found, being out and proud and ready for action.

'Mm, somebody needs fucking,' he said, loud enough for the recording equipment to pick up. 'What do you think?' He let his fingertips flutter over the swollen bead, never touching it in the way I craved.

'Please,' I whimpered.

'Didn't hear you.'

'Please,' I wailed.

'Please? I get that, but there's something missing, isn't there? Only girls who ask nicely get their pussies used, Sarah, you know that.'

He withdrew his hand from between my thighs and smacked at the soft inner flesh, several times, hard.

'Please, Sir,' I clarified, trying to push my bottom out invitingly, though the ropes curtailed my movements.

'OK. I'll just bring the camera closer. Maybe a side angle is best for this … hmm.'

He faffed around with the camera for so long I nearly exploded with frustration. My clit felt huge, hanging there waiting for him, while the heat all around it set fire to every nerve ending.

'That's it,' he said, swaggering up behind me.

He unbuttoned his trousers, pulled down his pants and took hold of me by the front of my thighs, nudging my pussy up to meet the head of his cock.

He went in swiftly and smoothly, my copious juices easing his way.

'There,' he said, holding the position.

I felt the tip of him rub against the end of the butt plug. I was double-stuffed, as full as could be. The short wiry hairs around the base of his cock re-ignited the ferocious sting of the switch cuts – he must have known this, because he swivelled his hips slowly, filling me with an intense combination of pleasure and pain that equalled total submission.

'Look at the camera, Sarah.'

I've seen that look many times when I've watched the film back. I always wonder what a stranger, viewing it without knowledge of me or Jasper or our dynamic, would make of it. I look the picture of defeated woe, yet I know that, in my heart, I am perfectly thrilled.

'Now tell the camera what's happening to you. In precise detail.'

'I'm tied to a tree,' I said slowly, fighting for breath. 'And I'm naked. I've just been whipped. My bottom is very sore. I have a plug up inside it, and my master's cock is in my cunt. I'm about to get fucked.'

'Beautiful. Perfectly scripted.' Jasper patted my flank in approval. 'And I think that's my cue.'

It wasn't the easiest or most comfortable way to get fucked, but Jasper knew what he was doing and he managed to hold me in a position that didn't wrench anything while he thrust inside me, jiggling the plug with each surge forward. I gripped my ropes for dear life and let him lift me slightly, so my feet were off the ground and my legs braced around his calves. He must have had amazing strength and stamina to maintain this position, but he did it brilliantly. Sparks of friction built and built while the butt plug added an exquisite element to proceedings. When the climax came, it would take my whole body, crown to toes, and the anticipation of it stopped up my breath and made my skin tingle.

'Take it, take it, take it,' he grunted.

'Please, Sir, may I come?'

'Louder!'

'Please, Sir, may I come?' I shouted it, hearing my voice ring through the wood.

'Yes.'

He nearly dropped me. I kicked and bucked so hard, my anal muscles clinging to the plug while I spasmed around Jasper's thrusting cock, that he swore and lurched forward, stumbling.

By the time I was wrung out, he had regained his footing, and he gripped me bruisingly hard for the last few strokes, growling in triumph when he filled me.

'Christ,' he said, panting, lowering me to the ground again. 'Thank God for weight training.'

He seized me by the chin and pushed his tongue, deep and possessively, into my mouth.

'You horny little bitch,' he whispered, letting me up for air. 'I'm adding you to my collection. You'd better catalogue yourself, love, because I own you, and you know it.'

I caught his mouth with mine and made him kiss me again. And again, and again.

Did he mean this? Did he want to keep me? Did I want to be kept?

He pulled out, leaving his spunk to trickle down my hot, sore thighs.

'You look beautiful,' he said. 'Fucking ravishing. And ravished.'

I wanted him to come back, come close, kiss me again, but he didn't.

He walked away.

By the time I looked around, to see what he was doing, he had gone.

'Jasper!' I called, but answer came there none.

So there I was, hanging from a tree, dripping with semen, plugged and whipped in the open. *The bastard.*

After ten minutes, I became genuinely anxious that he wasn't coming back. There had been an accident. He had taken an urgent call. He had fallen asleep.

147

The crackle of undergrowth lifted my heart and opened up my lungs for big breaths of relief.

'That was mean,' I called out. 'Really mean.'

The crackling stopped and I craned my neck round, but he was just beyond my range of vision.

'Please, Sir, could you untie me now? My arms are aching.'

'I don't know about that.'

My feet left the floor and I almost broke the branch in my efforts to twist around.

'Will!'

'Well, fuck me. Look what the bastard's gone and got himself. A willing little sex slave. I knew he'd got you into his kinks, but I didn't know what a pervy little slut you were. I'd have gone to town on you if I had.'

'Fuck off, Will. He'll be back any minute.'

'I'd rather fuck you than fuck off,' said Will.

I could hear the leer in his voice and I stiffened.

'Don't even think about it,' I hissed, as threatening as I could make it from my position of humiliating bondage.

'What would you do about it?' He moved closer, sucking in a breath. 'Ouch, that looks sore. Seriously, what are you doing with this guy? He enjoys hurting you. I don't get it.'

'I want him to. I like it.'

'And, to think, you didn't even know what a butt plug was …'

'Yes, I did.'

'And now you've got one stuffed up your bum. Did you have it in when he fucked you?'

'Just … fuck … off. Don't even think about touching me or I'll have Jasper on to you faster than –'

'Oh, stop it. I know he doesn't like to share his toys. I hope you aren't getting in too deep, though. It won't last. It never does.'

'Go away,' I said, but my resolve was weaker, shot down by his wounding words. I both did and didn't want to know what he had to say about Jasper's track record.

'He's a collector, love. You know that. And he isn't about to stop collecting. You're just another entry on the list.' He paused for a moment while I tried to ignore all the implications of this statement. Not listening. Don't want to know. Then he spoke again. 'Then again, you could just be the last. His style might just be cramped, pretty soon.'

'What do you mean?'

'Never mind. Look, Sarah, I appreciate your not telling him you'd seen me before. You could have got me in all kinds of trouble. Thanks.'

'I'll tell him about this.'

'Please … why don't I untie you and you can come with me? You should get away from him. Things are going to get sticky around here and there's no reason you should be involved.'

149

'Tell me what you mean.'

Rustling bracken foretold the reappearance of Jasper.

'Screw it,' muttered Will, taking to his heels. 'Screw you. And him.'

'Who were you talking to?'

Jasper appeared to my left, a curious, not altogether comfortable, smile on his face.

I took a deep breath.

'Will.'

'*Will?* The groundsman?'

I nodded.

'Please ... could you untie me.' A sudden gush of tears surprised me.

Jasper leaped up behind me and unknotted the rope, then he stood with his arms around me, tight and encompassing. My sore bottom rubbed against his jeans in a rather wince-inducing manner, but that wasn't why I was crying.

'What were you doing with Will?' he asked, the severity of his tone implying that he had gleaned completely the wrong idea. 'You know what I said when we got together.'

'No, not like that,' I sobbed. 'You can't think I'd cheat on you. I never would.'

'OK, OK.' He turned me round and let me water his chest, his hands in my hair. 'I'm sorry. I trust you. What was he doing here?'

'I don't know. He ... he seems to think something

bad's about to happen. But I don't know what. He was warning me.'

'What sort of something bad?'

I shook my head. 'He seemed to think he could tell me things about you that I wouldn't like to hear.'

'But he didn't say what they were?'

'No.'

Jasper held me at arm's length, frowning.

'Get the camera,' he said, fishing out his mobile from his pocket and jabbing at it.

I picked up all the equipment and trotted after him, clutching all the cold hardware to my bare chest. Walking wasn't easy – my legs were stiff, my bum still full of plug – but I barely noticed. I was too interested in Jasper's phone conversations.

The first one was obviously to Will.

'Whatever you've done, you're going to tell me what it is, now. I don't care what you've got on me. You could only have anything on me if you'd broken into my house and stolen my property. Is that what you did? So I should inform the police then? I don't give a shit. Bring it on. You can say what you like about me. I'm not a fucking politician or a royal – it's not going to do me any permanent damage. Right. I know what you've got then, and it reflects pretty badly on you. What's she ever done to hurt you? Damage limitation first, and then you'd better prepare yourself for a whole world of pain. Don't think

I'll ever let this go. I won't. But it's not me you'll have to worry about.'

'What's he done?' I asked nervously.

'He won't say for sure, but I think he's stolen a videotape of mine. An old one, from about twelve years ago. And he's given it to somebody – one of the newspapers.'

'What's the videotape?'

'The fucker,' he fumed. 'Look, I have to try and call around a few people first. I'll tell you when I've done that.'

A long and frantic conversation with his lawyer took us all the way up the house and beyond. I went upstairs to my room and dealt with the butt plug. Then I took a shower, dressed and came back down.

So this was a crisis. I felt a sense of dread, but also a weird kind of hope – as if this might finally bring our relationship into sharp focus and show me whether it was viable.

He was sitting in the biggest drawing room, hunched forward, hands steepled with fingertips over his mouth, when I found him. He didn't look up when I came in.

'So.' I spoke into strangely deadened air. 'What's going to happen?'

He watched me walk towards him. He didn't hold out a hand or anything, so I sat in the armchair. Acres of space seemed to lie between us, though it was only a couple of feet in reality.

'I don't know yet,' he said. 'My lawyer's making some calls, trying to see if he can spike it. If not, he'll have to shoot for an injunction. It might be too late. We'll just have to wait and see.'

'What's the video?'

He looked away from me, towards a large Fragonard painting on the wall, packed with merry creatures disporting themselves in green pastures. Just as we had been doing, not so long ago.

'Shit,' he said quietly. 'There's another call I have to make. I have to warn her.' He slapped his palm against his forehead. 'Fuck.'

'The videotape's definitely gone?'

'Definitely. Why didn't I burn it? God, why?'

'Jasper. I'm really worried. What's on it?'

'It's not *what's* on it so much. It's standard BDSM play, though it could be misinterpreted, of course. It's *who's* on it.'

'So who's on it?'

'Ava Rose.'

'Ava Rose! Who married the –'

'The King of Saxenland. Yes. Her.'

'Oh, bloody hell.'

Queen Ava had filled the void in the worldwide public appetite for beautiful royal women left by Diana's death. She had been the most photographed, most written-about, most idolised and most scrutinised woman in the world ever since her engagement to the European monarch was announced nine years before.

The presses, from Alaska to Australia, were going to explode with the heat of this story.

'Yeah,' said Jasper contemplatively. 'Bloody, as you say, hell. Look, if you want to get out of here before the circus starts –'

'No,' I said. 'I want to stay with you.'

He finally looked at me.

'I should send you home,' he said.

'I wouldn't go.'

He shook his head. 'Silly. But thank you. And now I really have to make that call. Would you mind …?'

I left the room, wishing I could stay and listen in to Jasper's hotline to royalty. I tried to cast my mind back and recall if I'd ever read something about him and Ava Rose seeing each other, but nothing sprang to mind. Surely it would have been in all the magazines. He was pretty popular in that hospital soap, and she was the hot TV presenter of the day. It must have been a purely sexual arrangement.

It won't last. It never does.

I sat on the stairs, then thought better of it and stood up, contemplating the dark wood panelling that stretched above me and on all sides, making a mental inventory of all the pictures and *objets* in the hall. There were loads, and I was still only halfway through when Jasper opened the living room door. He looked pale and a bit sweaty.

'That's done,' he said ominously. 'And at least there are better lawyers than mine on the case now. Let's go to bed.'

'Bed?' I stood up, confused. 'It's five o'clock in the afternoon.'

'The phone's going to ring like fury from now until tomorrow morning. We might as well grab what rest we can while it's quiet.'

Still exhausted from the open air activity, we lay in each other's arms, waiting. The waiting kept us awake, so we talked.

He told me all about his brief affair with Ava. They had bonded at some TV awards and quickly – accidentally – recognised their mutual interest in BDSM. They had made a pact to meet in secret and play scenes once a month. Jasper had promised to destroy the one film he had made, but somehow had never been able to bring himself to. The affair had ended when Ava met the Saxenlandish Prince.

'I should have burnt it there and then,' he groaned. 'I was a fool.'

'You weren't to know that Will was going to snoop around your private belongings,' I said.

'I should have been prepared for it. People pry; it's part of human nature. I was so careful with that cupboard. I kept it locked.'

'I think he must have some kind of master key.'

155

'I made him hand them all over when he left.'

'Well, he obviously had an extra one, or how would he have been able to keep breaking in whenever he fancied?'

Jasper turned to me with one eye open and I went cold all over, realising my mistake.

'Whenever he fancied? He was in here more than once?'

'Maybe,' I mumbled. 'Oh God. I'm sorry. I should have told you.'

'Told me what?' He had sat up straight now and his expression frightened me.

'I saw him once before. That day we had the picnic by the lake.'

'You didn't tell me.'

'I … I just didn't want to … make trouble.'

'Make trouble? What the fuck do you think *this* is? What did he do? What did he say?'

'He just made vague threats. Said he was going to get even and all that kind of thing. I thought he was just blowing off steam.'

'Well, you thought wrong, didn't you? Jesus Christ, Sarah.'

'I'm sorry,' I pleaded.

His cold fury had the better of him.

'Get out of here,' he said. 'I don't want you here. Go on.'

'I don't want to leave you –'

'I don't care what you want. You've had your fun. Now get out.'

It was difficult to leave the room in a dignified manner when I was buck naked and my backside scored with birch welts, but I tried my best. I only broke down in tears once I'd made it into my own little room.

I packed my bags and took them downstairs. The last thing I heard before I shut the front door was the shrill of Jasper's mobile phone.

I loaded my bags into the boot of my car and drove to the village. I almost carried on past the crossroads towards the motorway and home, but something made me park the car by the war memorial in the village centre and head into the pub.

A few enquiries were enough to get me Will's address, and I ran through the streets to the new-build development on the edge of the fields.

He was outside, watering the plants in his postage-stamp-sized garden when I pulled up at his gate, massively out of breath and bent double.

'Oh, look what the wind blew in,' he said, putting down his hosepipe and wandering over to the gate. 'You got out while the going was good, did you?'

'Why did you do it, you bastard?' I panted.

'Not a very nice way to greet your lover.'

'Ex-lover.'

He shrugged.

'Come in. I'll brew up.'

'Don't bother. I just want to see if I can stop it.'

He opened the gate and waved me down the path.

'Stop what?'

'This horrible thing you've done. Can't you contact whoever you gave the tape to and tell them you don't want to run it? Whatever they've paid you, can't you give it back? I'm sure Jasper could match whatever their offer was.'

'Yeah, yeah, Jasper the man. Gets what he wants, uses it, throws it away.'

Will's bitter tone made my heart sink.

'Take a seat,' he invited, once we were in his cramped living room.

I sat gingerly on the fake-leather sofa. The birch welts throbbed.

'It's not about Jasper. It's about the other person involved. Have you given a second's thought to the implications for her?'

'You?'

'No, you dingbat. Ava. Queen Ava.'

He looked through the window for a moment, his lips pinched.

'Listen, Will. I'll do whatever it takes to stop this happening. Is there anything I can do? Anything you want from me? I'll give it to you if you get that videotape back.'

Will stared.

'Christ, he's really got you well trained, hasn't he? Got you whoring yourself to save his skin. Gotta hand it to him.'

'No, you're wrong. He doesn't know I'm here. Besides, we're finished.'

'Finished? Really? So he did what he always does, then. Took his fill and pushed the plate away.'

'I don't know about that.'

There was a silence.

'He's called Ava's people. I imagine her lawyers will come down on you like a ton of bricks. This is so much more serious than simple theft.'

'The newspaper promised not to name me.'

'You think heavyweight international lawyers can't get past a worthless promise from a tabloid rag?'

'Shut up, Sarah. OK then. Let me fuck you the way he does and I'll see what I can do.'

I hesitated. I really didn't want this, and I didn't think it would make any difference anyway. If the tape was in the hands of the press, the game was over. Even if the lawyers got their injunction, it would leak out on to the internet at some point. It was inevitable. I'd been trying to appeal to Will's conscience. I'd failed.

'The way he does?' I said.

'Yeah. Why does he get to dominate you? You never let me treat you like that.'

'I didn't think it was your scene.' *I didn't want you that way. I didn't trust you. Turns out my instincts were right as well.*

'Bend over then, and I'll show you whether it's my scene or not, sweetheart.'

'I'm already a little ...'

'Yeah, I saw what he did to you, remember? But it's just a little pain, darling, and you like that.'

He'd grabbed hold of my wrist and pulled me up from the sofa.

I screamed and tried to wrench myself away, knocking an iPod speaker off the coffee table. We fell into a wrestling match that ended on the floor, me crying and gasping for breath, him swearing and pinning me to the ground.

'Do you like rape play?' he snarled, looming over me. 'I bet you do. You like it rough. No means yes and all that.'

'Get off me!'

'That's it, baby, that's the way to play the scene.'

'I mean it.'

'I bet you let *him* rape you.'

I kicked the coffee table again and something else fell off. From the corner of my eye I caught sight of Jasper's handwriting on the label. '*June 2000.*'

'It's the tape!' I exclaimed, struggling even harder to release myself from Will's grip. 'How come you've still got it?'

His fingers loosened and he looked over at the tape, distracted for just long enough for me to bring my knee up hard into his groin.

'Fuck!' he bellowed, toppling backwards, releasing me.

I snatched up the videotape and leaped up into the doorway, ready to slam it in his face if he tried to pursue me.

'Did you make a copy?' I asked.

He panted angrily for a few moments then muttered, 'No.'

'So what's it doing here?'

'I haven't sent it to anyone. I was bluffing. I wouldn't do that to Queen Ava.'

Words. Where were the words? Why wouldn't they come?

'I just wanted to teach Jasper Jay a lesson,' he said. 'Fucking high and mighty fucking twat. Just wanted to scare him and split you up.'

'But ... but ... he's been on to his lawyers and the press. Everyone's going to know there's some dodgy tape. God, I hope they haven't mentioned Ava's name! But I guess ... they wouldn't ... oh, sod this. I've got to go.'

I left Will trying to get back to his feet and catch me, but I had a good few yards' advantage and I flew back to the car, heart pounding.

I was almost too strung up to drive, my hands shaking and the road back to Jasper's estate seeming strangely

161

unfamiliar and out of focus, but I somehow got to the house without any collisions and sped up the drive. If it hadn't been for the gravel, I think my tyres would have actually squealed when I slammed on the brakes by the front door.

I dropped my key three times before I could wrestle it into the lock, but finally I rushed into the hallway and called for Jasper.

'Jasper! It's OK. I've got it. I've got the tape.'

I heard his bedroom door bang and his feet on the stairs. I prayed that his face wouldn't be that cold, dead-eyed version I'd last seen on him.

'What are you talking about? What are you doing here?'

He appeared on the landing. I proffered the videotape.

'This is it, isn't it?'

He rushed down and snatched it from me.

'God, I hope so,' he said, and took it into his office.

I followed him and looked over his shoulder as he fed the tape into one of his cameras and pressed play.

In the little screen, I could see only greyness at first, then a bed with cuffs attached to each one of its four posts, viewed through a doorway. There was a woman on the bed, but it wasn't until the end of a long tracking shot ending at the footboard that she became clearly and definitively Ava Rose. Despite the blindfold, it was obvious that those tethered wrists and ankles belonged to the Queen of Saxenland.

'This is it,' said Jasper, exhaling massively. 'Oh God. This is it. Shit. I think I'm going to have to sit down.'

He sank into his office chair and put his head between his knees.

I wanted to go over and rub his shoulders or perform some other action of a soothing nature. But perhaps that would draw attention to me and he'd remember that he'd sent me away.

Instead, I looked at the camera. The tape was still running, but fast-forwarded, so that Jasper and Ava played their scene at a comic speed. Cane strokes fell too quickly and there was much epic thrusting and thrashing. It looked like fun. I wondered if Ava had that much fun now.

When Jasper looked up, his eyes were bloodshot. I couldn't interpret the look on his face – was it anger, sadness, curiosity, contemplation, what?

'I've got some calls to make,' he said. 'Go and get us a brandy, love, would you?'

Love. I was his love again.

When I took the brandy in to the office, he was talking to his lawyer again in a low, urgent voice. He put the phone down and necked down a substantial slug of his drink.

'Is it going to be OK?' I asked, my voice coming out in a timid whisper.

'I hope so,' he said. 'My lawyer didn't ever tell anyone what he thought they had in their possession. So they don't know it's a sex tape. It's just an item of my property. They can guess, of course ... but the main thing is, Ava's name wasn't mentioned. Only mine.'

'Oh, that's great. So they don't really have a story and they'll probably just drop it?'

'Well, I suppose they'll think there's no smoke without fire and dig around in the dirt for a while. But they can dig all they like. That tape will be burnt.'

I nodded and waited for whatever was coming next. A fond goodbye? A word of thanks? A curt dismissal?

No. What came next was completely unexpected. He blinked and I could see a dark cloud of suspicion crossing his face.

'Wait a moment,' he said. 'How did you get this?'

'I went to Will's place and saw it in his living room.'

'How do I know you didn't make a copy?'

'*Me?*'

'How do I know you and him weren't co-conspirators from the start? You planned this. You let him into the house. You were fucking him all along.'

'Jesus, Jasper! No! You've got completely the wrong end of the stick!'

'It all makes sense,' he said, almost to himself. 'You found my stuff, you decided to make some money out of me. You gave him the tape. And now you're playing at saving the day, so I don't get my lawyers after you.'

'This is paranoia! Please stop it, Jasper. I had to fight him for this tape. I only did it because I love you.'

I held out my arms, covered now in fingermark bruising from my struggle with Will.

'Look!'

He looked, then turned his face away.

'Rough sex,' he muttered.

'No! Oh, God, he'd be loving this. This is what he wanted – to break us up and drive you mad.'

He had nothing to say to that.

'You'll see when the papers come out tomorrow,' I persisted. 'There'll be nothing. No scandal, no sex tape. Will said himself he wouldn't do that to Ava.'

'What a gent,' sneered Jasper, but a dim light seemed to be dawning.

'And I would never do anything to hurt you,' I said, more quietly, trying to turn every cell of my body into sincerity that would force its way from my words to his heart. 'Because I love you.'

'So you said.' He drained the rest of the brandy. 'But love's a tricky bugger, isn't it? I've seen it faked too many times. Sometimes for the camera. Sometimes not.'

'Oh, Jasper.' A flicker of real pain in his eyes made me move towards him.

He flinched.

'Don't. I know the lines by heart. All of them.'

'But they aren't always just lines. Somebody must have said they loved you and meant it. Surely.'

'I thought they did, once. I was wrong. I don't want to talk about love. I don't want to go through the disappointment again.'

'Somebody broke your heart.'

'If you want to put it that way, trite and unoriginal as it is.'

'Was it Ava?'

He slumped in his chair, then picked up the empty glass.

'I need more of this,' he said. 'Let's get out of here. In fact, let's build a bonfire and put this on top.'

He wrenched the tape from the camera and set off, glass in hand, towards the drawing room that held the brandy decanter.

Fortified with more firewater, we wandered outside, by the stables, and Jasper began building a pyre, composed of discarded brushwood and early fallen leaves.

'You know,' he said, raking more twigs towards the pile, 'perhaps I should add my whole collection to this. All those whips and cuffs and Victorian butt plugs.'

'No.' I was aghast. 'You don't mean that. Your collection is amazing. It would be criminal.'

He smiled, a tad grimly.

'Or I could just sell it on,' he suggested.

'But why? You've had so much pleasure from it. *We've* had so much pleasure from it.'

'It's all too risky. It's made too much trouble for me now. I'll burn it, go back to France and make my film.'

He set light to the uneven pyramid of extraneous matter and threw the videotape carelessly on top.

'*Ciao, bella,*' he said, but he turned away so I couldn't see his face.

'You really loved her, didn't you?' I said.

'Right, that stuff's for the tip. I'm going to throw it all on, piece by piece, cane by cane.'

'You bloody well aren't!'

He started to walk towards the house but I darted in front of him, barring his way.

'I won't let you,' I vowed. 'It's vandalism. I can't bear to see beautiful things being destroyed. You can throw me on that fire if you like, but don't you dare ruin that fantastic collection.'

He reached out to push me aside but I swung my fist really, really hard and hit him in the ribs.

I hadn't expected it to hurt him. I'm no fighter. But he grabbed himself, winded, and couldn't speak for a moment or two.

'I'm sorry,' I muttered. 'Sorry. I didn't mean to actually hurt you. Oh, God, perhaps I should just go.'

He reached out for me at that and grabbed me by my bruised forearms, which was startlingly painful. But he

167

hadn't intended to cause me pain, merely to pull me hard into his arms and cling on tight.

'Don't go,' he said in a strangled kind of voice. 'I'm a stupid twat. Don't leave me.'

I think he was crying, but I didn't look up. My cheek was crushed into his shoulder and his arms were like steel bands around me, the pressure threatening to pulp my ribcage.

When he let me go, I could feel my body rearranging itself into its former configurations.

'I'm sorry, Sarah,' he said, holding up one of my wrists and inspecting my bruises. 'Sorry I was paranoid earlier and sorry I'm so bad at this.'

'Bad at what?'

'Relationships.'

'I don't think you are.' I paused. 'Not *that* bad.'

He laughed.

'Come to the fire,' he said.

We sat propped up against the stable door and watched the flames flicker and jump. Every now and then, he refilled the brandy glasses.

'I did love her. You were right,' he said, once the last section of videotape had melted away. 'But she wouldn't go public about our relationship. I didn't really get it. She said it was because she didn't want the press attention but it turned out it was because she was waiting for something better to come along.'

'Something like a King?'

'Exactly like a King.'

'But it was twelve years ago,' I pointed out, as gently as I could. 'And she was just one woman out of a whole world.'

'I know. I know that in *here*.' He tapped the side of his head. 'But I can't make the message get through somehow.'

'You gave up on love?'

'Yeah. I thought I'd just have a series of sex partners instead. Keep it light. Play at it without stepping over the line.'

'It's about control,' I said.

'You think?' He stuck his tongue out at me. Yeah, I know it was obvious, but it was worth saying.

'Well, it is. You lost control when you fell for Ava. You don't want to lose it again. I can understand that. Loss of control is very frightening. When it isn't negotiated, that is. It's quite fun when you give it away.'

I quirked my lips at him.

'See, I don't like this,' he said, shaking his head. 'You know too much. And I might like you too much. It's not what I envisaged when I decided to seduce you.'

'You thought, a few weeks of fun ordering me about and then I'd move on when the cataloguing job was done?'

'A summer of submission,' he said. 'I know I sound heartless.'

169

I put my hand on his arm.

'I don't think you're heartless,' I said. 'But you have to accept that other people have hearts too. And they sometimes give them to you.'

'Keep them,' he said. 'I don't know what to do with them.'

I looked up at the stars.

'It'll be September soon.'

'And you'll fly away with the harvest moon.'

He put his arm around me.

'That's what you want, isn't it?' I whispered.

'It was.'

I leaned into his shoulder.

'What do you want now?'

'I want you to stay here. I want to keep you here, locked up in my attic, where you can't escape me.'

My heart was skipping beats all over the place, like a smudged CD. But I had to keep my head.

'I don't think that would go down very well at the South Coast Heritage Park.'

'The where? Is that where you're going when you finish here?'

'They've offered me a job, yes. In the Victorian House museum. It starts at the end of next month.'

He was silent for a moment, picking up my forearm and frowning at the bruises. He kissed each one, gently as a whisper.

'Bloody real people,' he muttered. 'Bloody real people with their real lives and real jobs and real feelings. Why can't you be one of my characters? Throw it all aside and give yourself to me?'

'You don't really want me to.'

'Yes, I do.'

'Maybe one day. But not now. It's too soon. I don't know you well enough, and you obviously don't know me well enough, or you wouldn't have accused me of conspiring to ruin your life with Will.'

'I'm sorry.' He looked away up to the stars, his brow knitted tight. 'I'm good at fucking up my own life, aren't I?'

'I didn't say I wanted to leave you. I don't want to leave you. I said I loved you and I do. I can't walk away now.'

'But you're going to. You're going to walk all the way to the South Coast pretendy-history place when you could come to France with me and load my clapperboard.'

'I'd love to load your clapperboard, Jasper, but it's not what I've always dreamed of.'

'And fannying about in Victorian houses is? Yes. I know. You're an awkward little specimen, aren't you?'

'Love doesn't have to be all or nothing, you know. You think that if I loved you I'd give up everything to be with you. But would you give up your directing career to be with me? Or would you try to find a way of doing both?'

171

He inhaled tetchily.

'You're so fucking sane,' he said. 'I can't argue with you. OK, Sarah. Whatever you want. However you want to play this. Just as long as I get to keep hold of you. That's what we'll do. All right?'

'You can keep hold of me for as long as you want.'

'Well, that's the best news I've had all day.' He bent to kiss my cheek and we watched the fire die.

'Better than …?'

'The best,' he repeated firmly.

He stood up and tried to pull me up after him, but his ribs obviously ached and he put a hand to them.

'Christ, woman, you pack a serious punch.'

'Sorry.'

'You realise I'm going to have to punish you for that?'

I tensed my sore bottom. Not tonight, I hoped.

He chuckled at my dismay and patted my bum proprietorially.

'I'll leave it a few days, I think,' he said. 'Give you plenty of time for anticipation. And me plenty of time for creative thinking.'

'Oh, God, I know all about your creative thinking.'

He opened the back door and ushered me into the house.

'You don't know the half of it, darling.'

Chapter Seven

One week later, I stood in one corner of Jasper's bedroom with my nose in the spot where the two walls adjoined.

I'd been there a while, and my attention was starting to wander, my eyes sliding towards the window and looking out at the brightness beyond. It seemed strange to be standing here like this, with a bare bottom and a cane propped between my cheeks, when outside the oblivious birds were singing and a careless sun shone.

That cane was supposed to focus my mind and make me concentrate on what was to come. I was focused all right, but distracted too by the tight clutch of my corset and the way it pushed my breasts almost all the way up into my face. Despite my Victoriana fantasies, I don't think I'd have coped with wearing one of these on a daily basis.

I had been listening for footsteps so long that my ears had tired, but every little tap or clock chime from downstairs made me jump. When he had placed me here, he had not said how long I would have to wait. Perhaps it would be hours. All I knew was that I was not allowed to move and that eventually that little crook handle resting in my cleft was going to be picked up and used in a way I wasn't going to like. At the time.

My thoughts drifted to the week that had passed. There had been very little in the way of kink but a lot in the way of lying in each other's arms and talking. And sex. Lots of that, if mostly of the vanilla variety. We were both exhausted and even Jasper's imagination needed a sabbatical sometimes. But now it seemed it was back and firing on all cylinders.

My body had relaxed a little during this reverie, but an unmistakable creak of the stair brought it back to full alert. Stomach in, shoulders back, legs straight. He was coming.

By the time he turned the handle, I could barely breathe and everything was churning.

The door opened quietly and for a horrible moment nothing was said, no sound heard.

'Did you move?' he asked in a low, measured voice.

'No, Sir.'

'Good.'

He came up behind me and the slender intrusive

presence between my arse cheeks was removed. Now I'm for it! I thought with a kind of dread exhilaration.

I felt its cold wooden tip tap my shoulder.

'Turn around,' he said.

When I caught sight of him, I had to clench my thighs to stem the flow of juices between them. I wanted to ask him where he had got the Victorian gentleman's outfit – was it his, or did he hire it? But that would be out of keeping with the scene. I would have to keep my questions for later. For now, I could content myself with drinking him in, and appreciating his attention to detail. A well-cut tailcoat, a paisley-patterned silk waistcoat, a fine lawn shirt, a perfectly tied stock. Cufflinks, fob watch, shiny, shiny shoes – the lot. And, of course, the cane, though this was not of the gold-topped walking variety.

I think he could tell I was impressed; the severity of his expression relaxed a little and he inclined his head in receipt of my wide-eyed tribute.

'Now then,' he said, stepping back and using his cane to trace my outline, from my shoulder, down my outer arm, up my inner arm, along the side and beyond. 'We have quite a catalogue of faults to address today, don't we, young lady?'

I bowed my head, trying not to shiver at the light touch of the cane at my hip.

'Yes, Sir.'

He brushed my thigh and tapped it, very gently, but it still made me jump forward on to my tiptoes.

'I would like to hear them from your lips,' he said. 'Before I come to deal with you.'

'I ... was not honest with you, Sir,' I whispered.

'Indeed you were not. You concealed a very important matter from me. A matter that could have led to devastation on an unacceptable scale.'

'I know, Sir, I'm sorry. Truly sorry.'

I flicked my eyelids up and tried to gauge his reaction to my penitence. Was it going to cut any ice at all? I doubted it.

'However sorry you might be, the gravity of the offence must be reflected in the chastisement, don't you agree?'

'Yes, Sir,' I sighed.

'Furthermore, there is the matter of your ... intemperate fist.'

I couldn't help a snigger at that. Hard as I tried to keep my mouth in a straight line and my breath even, it leaked out in spite of me.

'Is something amusing?' The tapping on my thigh increased in weight, conferring a series of warning little stings.

'No, no, not at all, Sir,' I rushed to correct my error. 'It was inexcusable behaviour.'

'It was, and I do not excuse it, as you will find out.'

I wrung my hands, my fingers clasping and unclasping

176

in front of my poorly concealed pubic triangle. I could try begging for mercy, but it seemed pointless.

'Please, Sir, how many?' I asked.

'You should not be asking how many, girl, you should be telling me how many you deserve and begging me to be thorough in the administering of them.'

God, he was good. I could barely keep still now, wanting to squirm with arousal.

'I cannot say, Sir,' I breathed. 'Perhaps … six?'

'Six? Six strokes?'

Oh dear. It would be more, then.

'I gave you six for the trifling matter of breaking a wine glass, if you remember. Didn't I?'

'Yes, Sir.'

'So you must surely agree that these serious transgressions merit a somewhat stiffer sentence?'

'I suppose I must, Sir.'

'I suppose you must. Hmm. Well, then. How shall we have you?'

He looked about the room, sizing up various items of furniture, assessing which would best assist him in the caning of his errant submissive.

'Over the footboard of the bed, I think.'

He put a pillow over the wooden top, to protect my stomach and ribs, and walked me by the elbow to the site of my forthcoming woe.

It was just the right height for the purpose. I had to

stand slightly on tiptoe, which he always liked, and my bottom jutted right out behind me, even when he made me spread my legs. I hoped this didn't mean he was going to aim any strokes at my inner thighs. He'd done that once before and it had been the worst pain by far.

But I didn't think I'd be in a position to negotiate today. I'd made a pact with myself that I would take everything he gave me up to the point where it became truly intolerable and I meant to stick to it.

Once my bottom was up and my palms flat on the covers, he opened the chest that contained his collection and took from it two lengths of silken cord. These he fastened around my wrists, securing them to the lower posts of the four-post bed.

'Don't want any hands getting in the way,' he explained, tightening a knot. 'I know you and your wandering hands.'

I'd put them over my bottom during one scene and accidentally ended up with a very sore set of knuckles. He was right, but I still wanted to protest. I stood no chance of eluding any part of my discipline now.

He repeated the procedure with my ankles, tethering them wide apart and binding them to the bottom of the end posts. I could barely move a muscle now, held absolutely fast and without the smallest area of wriggle-room.

This was going to be really, really hard.

'Now, I want your honest opinion, Sarah, and if I don't agree with it, there will be a penalty. How many strokes do you deserve?'

'What's the penalty, Sir?'

'I'll add an undetermined amount of strokes to the number I deem fitting. So you could end up with many more than you were originally in for.'

'Oh, I don't know!' I wailed. 'I can't think.'

'Try. Think about your misdeeds and try to translate them into a number.'

How many could I reasonably take without safe-wording? I tried to work it out. Six was horrible but bearable. The time he gave me ten, I nearly safeworded, but the time he gave me twelve, I started moving into a different headspace and felt like I could have taken more. Where was that magic number between 'STOP NOW!' and 'CARRY ON FOR EVER'? I thought it must be ten or eleven. So maybe ...

'Eighteen, Sir?' I hazarded.

'Eighteen?' He sounded impressed and I screwed up every nerve, desperately hoping I'd made the right call.

'That's quite an ordeal you've let yourself in for. I was going to say twelve. Ah well. Here.'

I saw the cane slither along the bed until he lifted it and held it to my face.

'Kiss it,' he murmured. 'Kiss the rod.'

I let my lips linger on the slender rattan, marvelling

at how such an innocuous-looking thing could inflict such exquisite agony.

Then he drew it away from me, moved behind and, without further ado, laid the first stroke, full across the middle of my bottom.

Oh, no. Eighteen was too much. Much too much.

'I can't,' I whimpered, but I didn't voice the safeword. Just wanted to warn him that it might soon get its first use. Without recourse to any kind of displacing movement, I just had to stay in my bonds and absorb the pain in its totality. And I would have to do it seventeen more times.

'How many is that, Sarah?' asked Jasper. 'You really don't want to lose count, you know.'

'One, Sir.'

I endured seven more shocking swishes, feeling the heat sear through me, holding myself at the very edge of my tolerance. I say I endured them, but in fact I begged for mercy throughout and made quite a yelping, pleading, gasping mess of myself.

The ninth stroke fell and I could take no more.

'Pax,' I squealed, then I started to cry. 'I'm sorry,' I sobbed. 'I'm so sorry. I let you down. I'm a crap submissive.'

'Hey, hey, shh,' he said, leaning over me and massaging my shoulders. 'No, you aren't. You aren't, Sarah. You've already taken more than a lot of girls can. Come on. Do you want me to untie you?'

I didn't know what I wanted. He was going to France the next day and I had been avoiding thinking about it but now it all loomed in front of me, unbearably. This was going to be over. My summer of submission was going to become an autumn of mundanity. That cane stroke had been my last for some time.

No. It couldn't be my last.

'I've changed my mind,' I said. 'I want more. I want you to carry on.'

Jasper's fingers pinched into my flesh.

'Don't say it if you don't want it,' he warned. 'I won't hold it against you, you know. It's fine.'

'I want you to finish. I want to take them all. Please.'

He kissed the back of my neck.

'All right. But safeword again if you have to. Promise me.'

'I promise.'

That tenth stroke was hell and heaven together, but I had new strength from somewhere and I knew I could keep going. By twelve, I was flying. I could take more and more and more. The pain was no longer hectic, shocking my body, but a constant erotic burn, feeding every nerve, filling me up.

I made it to eighteen and moaned out the count, ecstatic in victory.

Jasper put down the cane and knelt behind me.

'I'm so proud of you, love,' he said and he started

kissing along each throbbing line, holding me by my hips as if he thought I might move away, not that I possibly could. After kissing each criss-crossed welt, he buried his face between my thighs, sucking at the delicate flesh there before pushing his tongue over my clit and into my cunt, licking me thoroughly until I yelled for permission to come, which he gave with a hot, breathy command that made my clit tingle underneath it.

'While I've got you where I want you,' he said, rising again and probing between my tender bum cheeks, 'what about this arse? I'm thinking it's looking a little empty. What do you think?'

He prodded my tight ring. I could only clench, immobilised as I was.

'Take what you want,' I said.

'Oh,' he moaned. I could imagine his face, that little flicker of bliss that sometimes passed over it. 'I think I will.'

Then there was lubricant, cold and inexorable, then fingers inside me, then at last his hot, thick cock. How he fitted inside I couldn't work out; it seemed contrary to the laws of physics, but he spread and stretched me while I tried to fight but, too tightly bound, could only submit. And I didn't really want to fight him, but a little token resistance added enormously to our mutual pleasure.

I liked the feel of his linen shirt rubbing against my

smarting bum cheeks as he thrust, creating a raw friction that seemed to complement that of his cock in my tight passage. I wanted the brutality and force of it, the sense of utter possession that came with it. Every single part of my body was his; every orifice had accepted his mastery of it.

And now, as his fucking of my arse reached its height, he cupped a hand beneath my cunt and began to rub my clit.

'I want you to come with me in your arse,' he said. 'I want you to. You have my permission. Whenever you have to ...'

Climaxing with him inside my bottom seemed somehow like the most potently submissive act the universe had to offer – a true stripping down of all my pretences. An admission that I loved to be shamed and humiliated and used like a slut, and the more he did it, the harder I came.

'Yes, yes, yes,' he hissed. 'Feel that now.'

The orgasm seemed to go on and on, aftershocks and vibrations continuing to inhabit my senses. When he came, pumping into my back passage like a man possessed, I almost experienced a second wave.

It was perfect. My life, here, with him, was perfect. He knew what I was, and only he could nourish that part of me.

I was only semi-conscious when he pulled out and

untied me, then laid me on the bed. I was trembling all over and aching and sore and just, oh, it was the best feeling. I was floating.

He took off the period costume and lay with me in his arms, cradling me, making soothing noises and stroking my hair.

'When do you have to start your job?' he whispered.

'End of September. Four weeks.'

'Come to France with me.'

'I can't …'

'Surely you can spare a couple of weeks?'

Actually, I could. There was nothing to stop me going for a short holiday.

'I'd need to … tickets and passports and all that. And I'm supposed to be spending some time with my family …'

'You can spare a couple of weeks,' he repeated. 'If we part company now, you're going to have the worst sub drop of all time. I'd be neglecting to care for you properly. Come on. Have a fortnight's holiday in France. After that … we'll see.'

'Well, I suppose …' I thought about this. I was desperate to stay with him, on so many levels, but also afraid of leaving this place. It was as if we only existed here and our dynamic couldn't translate to the real world. And France was in the real world, or so I'd been told. I loved him here, with all my heart, but would I love him there? And there would be people everywhere, curious colleagues and beautiful actresses and clamorous paparazzi.

'Say yes. You have to say yes. I'm not leaving you like this.'

'Do you really want me in your real life?' It seemed absurd, too much to hope for.

'I want you. There aren't any conditions to it. I just want you. But you don't feel the same?'

No. I did. I felt exactly the same.

'I'll come,' I said. 'But I'm still taking that job.'

'Of course. Now get in the shower and I'll drive you up to get your passport. There's a lot of packing to do.'

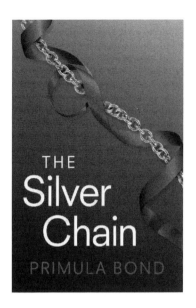

THE SILVER CHAIN – PRIMULA BOND

Good things come to those who wait…

After a chance meeting one evening, mysterious entrepreneur Gustav Levi and photographer Serena Folkes agree to a very special contract.

Gustav will launch Serena's photographic career at his gallery, but only if Serena agrees to become his companion.

To mark their agreement, Gustav gives Serena a bracelet and silver chain which binds them physically and symbolically. A sign that Serena is under Gustav's power.

As their passionate relationship intensifies, the silver chain pulls them closer together. But will Gustav's past tear them apart?

A passionate, unforgettable erotic romance for fans of *50 Shades of Grey* and Sylvia Day's *Crossfire Trilogy*.

GAME – JUSTINE ELYOT

The stakes are high, the game is on.

In this sequel to Justine Elyot's bestselling *On Demand*, Sophie discovers a whole new world of daring sexual exploits.

Sophie's sexual tastes have always been a bit on the wild side – something her boyfriend Lloyd has always loved about her.

But Sophie gives Lloyd every part of her body except her heart. To win all of her, Lloyd challenges Sophie to live out her secret fantasies.

As the game intensifies, she experiments with all kinds of kinks and fetishes in a bid to understand what she really wants. But Lloyd feature in her final decision? Or will the ultimate risk he takes drive her away from him?

Find out more at www.mischiefbooks.com

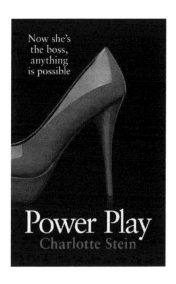

POWER PLAY – CHARLOTTE STEIN

Now she's the boss, everything that once seemed forbidden is possible…

Meet Eleanor Harding, a woman who loves to be in control and who puts Anastasia Steele in the shade.

When Eleanor is promoted, she loses two very important things: the heated relationship she had with her boss, and control over her own desires.

She finds herself suddenly craving something very different – and office junior, Ben, seems like just the sort of man to fulfil her needs. He's willing to show her all of the things she's been missing – namely, what it's like to be the one in charge.

Now all Eleanor has to do is decide…is Ben calling the kinky shots, or is she?

Find out more at www.mischiefbooks.com

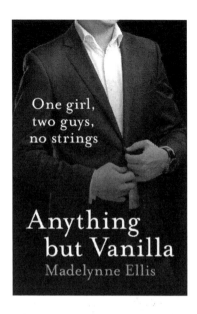

ANYTHING BUT VANILLA
MADELYNNE ELLIS

One girl, two guys, no strings.

Kara North is on the run. Fleeing from her controlling fiancé and a wedding she never wanted, she accepts the chance offer of refuge on Liddell Island, where she soon catches the eye of the island's owner, erotic photographer Ric Liddell.

But pleasure comes in more than one flavour when Zachary Blackwater, the charming ice-cream vendor also takes an interest, and wants more than just a tumble in the surf.

When Kara learns that the two men have been unlikely lovers for years, she becomes obsessed with the idea of a threesome.

Soon Kara is wondering how she ever considered committing herself to just one man.

Find out more at www.mischiefbooks.com

Printed in Great Britain
by Amazon

38679417R00110